The Watcher

Ed Adams

a firstelement production

Ed Adams

First published in Great Britain in 2021 by firstelement
Copyright © 2021 Ed Adams
Directed by thesixtwenty

10 9 8 7 6 5 4 3

A CIP catalogue record for this book is available from the British Library.

ISBN 13: 978-1-913818-20-3

eBook ISBN: 978-1-913818-21-0

Printed and bound in Great Britain by Ingram Spark

rashbre
an imprint of firstelement.co.uk
rashbre@mac.com

ed-adams.net

Jump

Imagination is everything.
It is the preview of life's coming attractions.

Thanks

A big thank you for the tolerance and bemused support from all of those around me. To those who know when it is time to say, "Step away from the keyboard!" and to those who don't.

To Julie for understanding that only comes with really knowing.

To thesixtwenty.co.uk for direction.

To the NaNoWriMo gang for the continued inspiration and encouragement.

To Topsham, for being lovely.

To the edge-walkers. They know who they are.

And, of course, thanks to the extensive support via the random scribbles of rashbre via
http://rashbre2.blogspot.com
and its cast of amazing and varied readers whether human, twittery, smoky, artistic, cool kats, photographic, dramatic, musical, anagrammed, globalized or simply maxed-out.

Not forgetting the cast of characters involved in producing this; they all have virtual lives of their own.

And of course, to you, dear reader, for at least 'giving it a go'.

Books by Ed Adams include:

Triangle Trilogy		About
1	The Triangle	Dirty money? Here's how to clean it
2	The Square	Weapons of Mass Destruction – don't let them get on your nerves
3	The Circle	The desert is no place to get lost
4	The Ox Stunner	The Triangle Trilogy – thick enough to stun an ox
		(all feature Jake, Bigsy, Clare, Chuck Manners)
Archangel Collection		
1	Archangel	Sometimes I am necessary
2	Raven	An eye that sees all between darkness and light
3	Card Game	Throwing oil on a troubled market
4	Magazine Clip	the above three in one heavy book.
5	Play On, Christina Nott	Christina Nott, on Tour for the FSB
6	Corrupt	Trouble at the House
7	Sleaze	Autos, Politics, Gstaad
		(all feature Jake, Bigsy, Clare, Chuck Manners)
Big Science Textbook		
1	Coin	Get rich quick with Cybercash – just don't tell GCHQ
2	An Unstable System	Creating the right kind of mind
3	The Watcher	We don't need no personal saviours here
4	Jump	Some kind of future
5	Pulse	Want more? Just stay away from the edge
Blade's Edge Trilogy		
1	Edge	World end climate collapse and sham discovered during magnetite mining from Jupiter's moon Ganymede.
2	Edge Blue	Earth's endgame, unless…
3	Edge Red	An artificially intelligent outcome, unless…
4	Edge of Forever	Edge Trilogy

About Ed Adams Novels:

Triangle Trilogy		About
1	Triangle	Money laundering within an international setting.
2	Square	A viral nerve agent being shipped by terrorists and WMDs
3	Circle	In the Arizona deserts, with the Navajo; about missiles stolen from storage.
4	Ox Stunner	the above three in one heavy book.
		(all feature Jake, Bigsy, Clare, Chuck Manners)
Archangel Collection		
1	Archangel	Biographical adventures of Russian trained Archangel, who, as Christina Nott, threads her way through other Triangle novels.
2	Raven	Big business gone bad and being a freemason won't absolve you
3	Card Game	Raven Pt 2 – Russian oligarchs attempt to take control
4	Magazine Clip	the above three in one heavy book.
5	Play On, Christina Nott	Christina Nott, on Tour for the FSB
6	Corrupt	Parliamentary corruption
7	Sleaze	Autos, Politics, Gstaad
		(all feature Christina Nott, Jake, Bigsy, Clare, Chuck Manners)
Big Science Textbook		
1	Coin	Cyber cash manipulation by the Russian state.
2	An Unstable System	Creating the right kind of mind
3	Jump	Some kind of future
4	The Watcher	From the Big Bang to the almost Almighty Whimper
5	Pulse	Sci-Fi dystopian blood management with nano-bots
Blade's Edge Trilogy		
1	Edge	World end climate collapse and sham discovered during magnetite mining from Jupiter's moon Ganymede.
2	Edge Blue	Endgame, for Earth – unless?
3	Edge Red	Museum Earth – unless?
4	Edge of Forever	Edge Trilogy

Ed Adams Novels: Links

Triangle Trilogy		Link:	Read?
1	Triangle	https://amzn.to/3c6zRMu	
2	Square	https://amzn.to/3sEiKYx	
3	Circle	https://amzn.to/3qLavYZ	
4	Ox Stunner	https://amzn.to/3sHxIgh	
Archangel Collection			
1	Archangel	https://amzn.to/2Y9nB5K	
2	Raven	https://amzn.to/2MiGVe6	
3	Raven's Card	https://amzn.to/2Y8HLgs	
4	Magazine Clip	https://amzn.to/3pbBJYn	
5	Play On, Christina Nott	https://amzn.to/2MbkuHl	
6	Corrupt	https://amzn.to/2M0HnOw	
7	Sleaze		
8	An Unstable System	https://amzn.to/2PRJciF	
Big Science Textbook			
1	Coin	https://amzn.to/3o82wmS	
2	An Unstable System	https://amzn.to/2PRJciF	
3	Jump	https://amzn.to/3kTFWjg	
4	The Watcher		
5	Pulse	https://amzn.to/3qQIBvL	
Edge of forever Trilogy			
1	Edge	https://amzn.to/2KDmYOW	
2	Edge Blue	https://amzn.to/2Kyq9au	
3	Edge Red	https://amzn.to/2KzJwjz	
4	Edge of Forever	https://amzn.to/3c57Ghj	

TABLE OF CONTENTS

Champion Angel

Throw up your voice but not your mind
While them agents of change go monopolize
Their colours and their faces are just shades of the same
All lost in the game.

And we don't need no personal saviours here
Just a warm hearth and water. It's purely biological.
No posturing mannequin man or woman
Shall receive my hand.

Among all you angels is a champion angel
Among all you devils, there's a free soul
Up from the disenfranchised, the engine cries
Up from the circle there's a hole.

The child insubordinate disrupts the pecking order
So go marry young while you can
'Cause the weave of the rug and the cut of the throne
Testify before the ocean's open hand.

I promise you this promise we are not alone
But why is it I alone that promise this
Deny the forces that would hurry men
If you still can.

We come now to a fracture in the road
Here time has taken her toll
The endless freezing and the thawing of the heart
Would eventually divide us apart.

What's that you found in the pocket of your coat?
Looks like a small sentiment that she wrote
Don't be my personal saviour I would not be saved
I chose to walk alone.

We come now to a fracture in the road
Here time has taken her toll
The endless freezing and the thawing of the heart
Would eventually divide us apart.

Jocelyn Jager Adams / Benjamin Knox Miller / Jeffrey Carl Prystowsky

Dragon Lines Campfire

We meet at Point Reyes, a little to the north-west of San Francisco. A quiet scenic spot, where you'd make a fire on the beach and look out towards the Pacific as the sun sets.

It was a convention that we'd always meet at an intersection of ley lines, and this point was a doozy.

It was Limantour's idea to call us together. Just four of us. That's Drake, Tomales, Limantour and me. The ones we knew about with a stake in the future of Earth. I thought it amusing that Limantour had chosen a kind of Grand Central Station of ley lines for our meeting.

Tomales commented about the ley lines. She stood, balanced upon a tall rock, her hiking boots and three colour swirly shorts (brown, orange, and muted cream) offset with a long-sleeved red tee shirt over which she wore a short-sleeved pink tee. The colours offset her smooth brown skin well.

She begins, "Human ancestors knew about these lines for thousands of years. The native Indians of the United States used to call the ley lines spirit lines and their

Shamans used to use the electro-magnetic energy in these lines to help them contact the spirits. They even designed their medicine wheel on the spirit lines, as they knew these lines followed a straight round line. How did they know about these lines and the energies that they give off? The answer's simple: the sky gods told them."

Hold that thought about the sky gods.

We look up in the air as four silent brown pelicans flew along the edge of the shoreline.

Limantour continues the conversation. She wears a dark sailor costume, small top, red scarf in a vee and pleated skirt. Today, this mistress of chaos sports ginger bobbed hair.

"European druids called them mystical lines. In Wales, they used the same name as eastern countries; they called them dragon lines - the red dragon - Y Ddraig Goch - overturned the white dragon of the Saxons. And we know Eastern countries called them dragon lines as the sky gods flew in dragons along these lines. "

"Just like we do now?" asks Tomales, "In our dream-like state?"

Limantour replies, "Yes, the aboriginal people of Australia even called these lines 'dream lines'. They claim that knowledge passed on to them from the sky gods. That'll be us, I guess."

I shivered. I was aware of a recurrent dream in my downtime. It featured a gigantic serpent with gaping jaws which was always just a few steps behind me.

Drake in his khaki 'I'm going camping' look adds, "And

the lines link well. Throughout history, all megalithic structures were built on top of ley lines."

A few sparks from the campfire popped and spiralled up into the air. Drake knew how to make a good fire.

He continued, "From the pyramids of Giza to Stonehenge, Notre Dame, Solomon's Temple, Parthenon, Oracle of Delphi, Rennes Le Chateau, Ziggurat, the Vatican, DC Capitol, Mecca, Agia Sophia, Aztec Pyramids, Bermuda Triangle, Coral Castle, even Nikola Tesla's lab."

"I think we know too much," I interrupted, thinking about ley lines and trade routes.

Drake laughed and continued to fiddle with the fire. We all knew he could just wave to start it, but he proved that he still knew the primitive ways.

There was a crackling, and I saw the air de-mosaic. As the ripple subsided, I recognised Abbott appear on a rock. I'd known Abbott for a long time, but he diverted toward the counterforces in nature. Think of the four riders of the Apocalypse. He would be a supporter of all of them. Dressed in a black tee shirt, black shirts, and black sneakers, I hoped this was not a sign. Abbott from the dark.

He spoke, as if already in the conversation, "I think of all of the obelisks. Humans obsess over pointy things. Many of the sections where two or more ley lines intersect are marked with obelisks, such as Washington DC monument, Vatican Courtyard, and Cleopatra's Needle in Central Park."

"Even the one in London, England," I added.

"Although Cleopatra's Needles have all moved, I guess two out of three remained on a ley after they were re-sited," said Tomales. She was unwrapping a small backpack. I guessed she'd brought food along.

Four large gulls overhead this time. Swooping, noticing the food potential but staying aloof.

Tomales ignored the birds and continued, "Those electromagnetic lines of the Earth are its veins and receive its energies from the sun that connects and affects every living thing on this planet. Humans are surrounded by electrons, and through these auras and by the activation of the seven energy chakras the humans still have potential to connect with their higher self. Remember the golden halos depicted on all spiritual figures throughout history?" She made a triangle shape with her hands.

Limantour flashed a smile, "Fascinating though this is, let's get back to the main purpose. Thank you all for coming.

"I'm going to propose another Intervention."

The Intervention

Now, as we Watchers all knew, Interventions were strictly off-limits. Lepton, who had inadvertently sped up the introduction of light, had to pay by being secluded for the rest of eternity, although he did figure out a way around that difficult situation.

There had only been a handful of Interventions in all the universe's 13.8 billion years, and I wasn't sure I was ready to take part in one of them.

Another intervention by Leonardo, had occurred back in the 15th Century. Parachutes, fighting vehicles, hydrodynamics, helicopters, revised astronomy. A series of holistic system theories, so ahead of their time that they were often overlooked. Leonardo wasn't a Watcher though; he was a Wakener. But he showed the defect of not having a universal compelling event.

Compelling event? Something that galvanises the discovery provided towards its implementation.

Limantour begins, "You've done the math? You can all see that we are approaching an Earth endgame?"

I looked at others - who were all nodding. This was a

truly compelling event. Do something or Earth goes horribly wrong. Overpopulation, energy and food shortages, climactic decline.

Tomales jumps down from the rock. "Yes, I estimate it is something like a few hundred years - probably less - before the entire planet gets destroyed in another climate catastrophe."

Drake adds, "Yes, and this time there's no passing asteroid to take the blame."

Limantour next, "Tomales and I have been looking at other options. Minimal interventions that could turn all of this around."

"Like what?" asks Abbott, "Even that global pandemic didn't give the humans a hint that things were bad."

"We need to turn it on its head," says Tomales, "Instead of a threat, give them something to grasp at, to change behaviour."

"It'll take a long time," replies Abbott. "Probably one evolutionary cycle. That is too long."

"We were thinking about a discovery," says Limantour, "One that speeds up their thinking,"

"Oh, yes?" asks Drake. "What kind of discovery?"

"Magnetite," answers Tomales, "It could solve so many of their problems. I talked to Lekton about it."

"Lekton?" asks Drake, "But I thought he wasn't welcome anymore?"

Tomales answers, "Yes, but he can report on the future. Remember, he is one of us that can go forward and backward through time."

"He's in a different, dark, room, for sure," answers Limantour, "And he told Tomales about magnetite."

"Huh?" I ask. "The nearest magnetite source is right out at Jupiter, and they haven't discovered it yet, let alone worked out how to make it work for them?"

I wonder how I even knew this. The bad dream hotline must have been sending me messages.

Tomales continues, "That's where asteroid (153814) 2001 WN5 comes in. It's more than a Navajo flying rock. It was once part of Ganymede, the largest moon of Jupiter. If we tilt Hubble Four just a degree or so, it will collide with the asteroid and send back data about the extent of Magnetite available. Magnetite which could be a lasting clean source of power for the Earth."

She kicked the fire, and more sparks rose into the air.

"Okay, but what about the law of unintended consequences?" asks Abbott.

"I hear you, but I think this is for the greater good. The most that would happen is a few timespace ripples from the impact. It is hardly going to start a chain-reaction," answers Limantour.

"We don't even need to touch the Earth for this to work," says Tomales, "We can hardly be accused of Intervention when it is so indirect." She looked around at us all. Limantour was drawing something with a stick in the sand. A circle with a diagonal line through it, over to the left-hand side.

"Here," she says, "The asteroid ((153814) 2001 WN5 passes within 250,000 km of the Earth. During the close approach, it should peak at about apparent magnitude 6.7, and will be visible in binoculars."

"If we tip Hubble Four ever so slightly, we'll have a direct course and the Hubble's own detectors will soon enough to pick up on the mineral composition."

"But aren't we forgetting something?" asks Abbott, "Earth does not understand about magnetite and its ability to make clean, powerful energy from lightweight structures."

"Okay, that is part two," answers Limantour, "We'll need to send in a few shards containing knowledge for the humans."

"I thought this was a simple plan?" asked Abbott." Now we have an asteroid collision and a rain of knowledge-shards hitting Earth?"

"Yes, the knowledge-shards were a later embellishment of the plan by Lekton, but I'm afraid they are an essential part," explains Tomales.

"And I suppose you know where to find sufficiently advanced civilisations that already know about magnetite mining?" asked Drake.

Limantour answers, "Yes, we had to find an exoplanet, and there is one on the Norma Arm of the Milky Way. They have the knowledge, but it would come in a bundle with several other discoveries, which cannot be easily separated."

"And I guess it's somewhere between 45,000 and 60,000 light years away?" asks Drake.

"More or less, " says Tomales, "Although remember we can manipulate time, at least going forward. Using travel time of a light year per second it is a 2000 second round trip or just over thirty-three Earth minutes, plus time at the far end for negotiation and so on. Call it a day altogether.

We all looked at one another. By tomorrow, we could have the secret of how to stop Earth from crashing headlong into oblivion, based upon a rather simple sounding plan by created by Lekton and replayed by Limantour and Tomales.

"But," I start, "There's so many things that could go wrong!"

"Faint heart never won fair ambition, " answers Limantour. "Has Earth taught you nothing?"

The others laughed. I sense they have already bought into the plan.

I looked toward the sky. The birds have all gone. It was the embers of sunset. So pretty, it would be a shame to lose this. I realised Limantour and Tomales had chosen this time for its theatricality.

"So do we get some of those shorts too?" I ask.

Opening

But I should wind back.

This is a history of the Universe kind of deal. The Earth doesn't even feature for the first 8 billion years. But I was there from the start and so were some of my dimensionless associates.

The first few moments were intensely interesting, then the next few billion years were screamingly boring. And the next couple after that. It didn't really pick up until about 50,000 years ago, when the ice was finally retreating from the northern hemisphere of Earth for the last time.

I could edit my time exposure for most of it. Like 21st century streaming devices, I could fast forward over the dross and freeze frame and play when something interesting appeared.

And some of you know that I could go forward through time, but I've not yet discovered any way to back-track, so I've had to make the most of any specific exposure to events.

Don't get me started on the Morrison premise, that we can only travel backward in time because it is only the past which we have experienced. Or that of Amis, with a secondary consciousness apparently living within. Even something like Kurt Vonnegut's Slaughterhouse Five with Billy Pilgrim watching bombs being retrieved by American bombers un-bombing Dresden. We all know it is the film being run backwards. Maybe also 'from swerve of shore to bend of bay' in the opening paragraph of Finnegan's Wake, obliquely denoting the curving of time.

Yes, we Watchers have time to browse most things.

Of course, I'm invulnerable, but not in a freaky-deaky superhero kind of way. It's just a function of my existence as a Watcher. We are all made of stars and that has a cosmic enough ring to it. My star turned out to be a planet, and it is the one known as Earth. They say every Watcher is given something specific, but I think it was a more chaotic allocation in the first phase of the so-called Big Bang.

Yes, I've been around for 13.8 billion years through the coming of the elements and the galaxies and the planets.

Look up to a dark part of the sky and in human science you'll see the remnants of the Big Bang rushing towards us all. Deep time and wide time, we live in both surrounded by dark energy and the conical curves of space in the humans' metaverse.

That's where I get a bonus pass because I can see gravity as a part of hyperspace. Most human minds can't comprehend this hybrid, heterotic disturbance of fundamental objects and think of it as something from a nightmare.

But on some levels, the dream is real.

Scientists talk about monster moonshine and cosmic strings. They are onto something, but their own mathematics have difficulty expressing it. Thus, the monstrous moonshine can refer to the perceived craziness of the relationship between M and the theory of modular functions expressed through a hyperbolic plane of prime factors.

Excuse the mathematics. Some say there is still a bottle of bourbon riding on discovering the proof.

To me and those like me, it really doesn't matter. We've seen the start of the universe, lived through billennia of emptiness and now that it is all getting genuinely exciting, we can see toward another event horizon as the Earth burns up through over-population and over-consumption.

We Watchers are not too impressed that the show which never ends will one day soon run out of content.

The thing is the scientists got it wrong. Their theory of the start of the universe is about as probable as the story of a world on the back of four elephants perched on the shell of a giant turtle. The human mathematics looks plausible, but someone should properly examine the big numbers needed to make everything work.

Yes, human mathematics needs around a decillion degrees Celsius to explain the start of the universe. That's a 10 with 33 zeros after it.

10,000,000,000,000,000,000,000,000,000,000,000.

Of course, the drop off from this number would release huge amounts of energy as it plummets in less than a second to a quadrillion and then to a trillion, billion and finally the temperature of the sun, some 6,400 degrees Celsius. These convenient assumptions written in by earnest straight-faced scholars reverse engineer a lie.

But these big numbers are not new, and Amedeo Avogadro had a go at calculating the number of particles of molecules, atoms, or ions in samples of compounds. But he and Stanislao Cannizzaro used a dimensionless number - still called the Avogadro number - to express the number of particles in one mole.

Dimensionless numbers: now we are getting somewhere.

Such a look into mathematics becomes a distraction. Turn the handle, crank the sums and however implausible it seems, if the numbers say so, then what can the scientific community do except believe? They have followed their thought using the guiderails of an incomplete mathematical system.

It is just like when the world was supposed to be flat, or the scientists thought that the sun orbited the Earth.

Yes, the cosmic dealer smiles all the time within his darkened room. He doesn't let on that there are other darkened rooms next door. You just must think of them.

I repeat.

Other darkened rooms, with different frames of reference. Lepton may have stumbled upon Light, but only in one of the frames of reference.

At least one of these dark areas of deep shadow contains a key to explain what happens when supergravity exerts its presence.

In string theory, a brane is a physical object that generalizes the notion of a point particle to higher dimensions. Branes (derived from the descriptions of a 2-dimensional membrane) are dynamic objects which can propagate through spacetime according to the rules of quantum mechanics. They have mass and can have other attributes such as charge.

How cool is that? Think of parallel universes.

The wrinkle in human thinking is that although multiple branes exist, it is not possible to travel between them.

Limited human thinking again, which conveniently misses the point? You can't come into my dark room if you are already in your own different one. That film-maker Kubrick had a go at explaining it, based upon the writings of Arthur C. Clarke, but it flew right over most people's heads as they said, "I don't understand what that was about."

Imagine one of those novelty celluloid fish and how they distort with a hand's heat to tell one's fortune. With the fish we get humans imposing rules, written on the explanatory packet. Jealousy, Indifference, Love, Fickleness, Passion, Death. For a 'brane we are not given the rules like with a celluloid fish, but instead we are given a D-Brane world volume which sets the outer limits of possibility, like a big gauge running from -100 to +100. That's the frame of reference.

So come into another darkened room away from the constraints of mathematics and there's a whole other way to view things.

Maybe the universe was a freak occurrence of supergravity, whose ripple was larger than expected and broke through spacetime pushing the rubble of an alternative universe with it? I should declare an interest. I know something of supergravity.

Or maybe gravity left the room entirely, taking away the tight binding of everything and throwing it across space like toys from a pram?

Even in the theological and spiritual version, where Earth is created, then Lucifer runs amok, Earth gets judged and then is ruined. This causes a re-boot and another six unknowable days to create what becomes an Earth 2.0?

See the frames of reference? Traditional science, new science, theology. Suspend disbelief as one moves between each of the rooms.

Now I could fast-forward through the first half-billion years of Earth, after the Big Bang, when Earth was still covered in water. To a time of tiny mammals, ancestors of humans, and how they took advantage of the disappearance of the great lizards, or dinosaurs.

Big Bang and Beyond

I said I could fast forward over everything, but I'll pause awhile.

I won't start with humans. I'll rewind back to the beginning of their scientific belief system.

I think the grounded Tomales, and the chaos known as Limantour agree with me about the universe and Earth formation, but I'm not so sure about the analytical and serious Drake and the increasingly dark Abbott.

To be honest, I think Abbott (even beyond his clothing) is showing signs of defection. He has recruited two whom he refers to as Cardinal and Bishop and I'm certain they are making a play to rule a newly formed Earth Council.

Those are not the moves of a Watcher.

Something about the Earthside scientific belief system: Before time, there were four known fundamental interactions or forces—first, the outrider known as gravitation, and later the two electromagnetic forces with their weak and strong interactions; then there is the expansion of space itself and the super-cooling of the still immensely hot universe because of cosmic inflation.

That's a big one. Cosmic Inflation. It is how human science explains the aftermath of the Big Bang. How all the universe gets set to a temperature at one time, to put it into equilibrium.

I don't think so. A space so vast that equilibrium is set faster than the speed of light. Someone needs to keep a watch over those human scientists, bending logic to suit their explanations.

I suppose we could view it that the two prevailing electromagnetic forces brought me and my kind into being. A quirk of physics and the small ripples flooding across an undetected universe. These ripples were in a different dark room from the physicists and mathematicians. Ripples that were the basis of the large-scale structures that formed much later.

Stages of the very early universe are understood to differing extents. The earliest parts are beyond the grasp of practical experiments in particle physics and can only be explored through other means.

Stay with me as I describe the human view of the start of the universe. The kind that floppy-haired earnest-looking physicists describe over waves of growling bass-line synthesiser music. I'll add the bongs where suppositions should be challenged.

We get the first trillionth of a second of cosmic time (Bong!), riding the Planck epoch and experiencing a super-heated starting point, with an estimated temperature of 10^33 degrees Celsius. (Bong!) I couldn't be physical during this, (who could?) and I would need a super-fast power of observation to see events that would otherwise pass in a blink.

Then, Time unpacks itself (Bong?). A convenient magic.

Then the second stage, also within minute fractions of the first second (Bong!). The Grand Unification Epoch, when the force of gravity separated from the three other fundamental forces, and the earliest particles (and anti-particles) were created (Bong - we should not discount gravity's effect on the whole creation process). Gravity separation allowed the formation of the 'branes which permeate alternate realities.

See what I said about gravity as the outrider.

I could handle all of this in my consciousness. I was equipped from the very start to handle metaverses, the non-persistence of gravity and the curious dilation of time. The fundamental force ripples that flooded the early universe became my friend and I, and the others like me, could adapt our own perception to appreciate what was happening.

And now, we could all detect time and gravity in this new and very particular dark room. As Watchers, we had been imbued with a unique gift to ride out the event horizon. We would exist for as long as Time existed,

On to the third stage, also within minute fractions of the first second (Bong!) It was the Inflationary Epoch which was triggered by the separation of the strong nuclear force.

We'd now gained a universe as it underwent an extremely rapid exponential expansion, known as cosmic inflation. The size of the universe during this tiny fraction of a second (Bong!) increased to around the size of a small insanely hard apple. And particles remaining from the Grand Unification Epoch, comprising hot, dense quarks, become distributed thinly across the universe.

As a Bong! to all of this, spacetime ripples would make an altogether plausible alternative theory.

Instead, sticking with Earth-science explanations, as the strong nuclear forces separated, particle interactions created large numbers of exotic particles and Higgs bosons in the Electro-weak Epoch. The Higgs bosons slowed down these particles and attributed mass to them, allowing a universe that was made entirely out of cosmic radiation to support particles with mass. This is when things became tangible rather than simply riding phase distortions.

Even now, Higg's boson isn't fully understood and additional theories like gauge invariance and spontaneous symmetry breaking have been wrapped around it. It is to the extent that analogies are used to describe it. That gets a Bong! from me. Think of a shady politician's accounts with a few balancing items to make everything tally.

Still in that first moment and we get the Quark Epoch, when quarks, electrons and neutrinos formed in large numbers as the temperature of the Universe cooled off to below 10 quadrillion degrees Celsius (Bong), and the four fundamental forces assume their present forms.

Or three of them do, with gravity as an outrider. Quarks and anti-quarks annihilated each other with contact, but in a process known as baryogenesis, a surplus of quarks survived and ultimately combined to form the first chemical matter.

We were experiencing the birth of tangible matter, admittedly still from the confines of one darkened room.

It's all about perception.

The Hadron Epoch followed, still within this first second of the Big Bang (Bong!). During this epoch, the temperature of the infant primordial universe cooled to around one trillion degrees Celsius (Bong).

Okay, CERN's Project ALICE are now thought to have 'momentarily' cooked up 5.5 trillion degrees Centigrade crashing gold nuclei at near light speed. That's hotter than the centre of the sun, by 250,000 times.

This super-hot Hadron Epoch was enough to allow quarks to combine to form hadrons such as protons and neutrons. Electrons colliding with protons fused to form neutrons and give off massless neutrinos, which continue to travel freely in space to this day at around the speed of light.

Now, this is where I should introduce my associate Lepton. He, like me, is a Watcher, although he graduated on to other things.

Lepton was trying to free himself. He could see it was a very long one-way trip along Earth's timeline and wanted to be able to exercise greater freedom to roam.

So, he decided to intervene. That is a strict no-no for all of us Watchers. Don't interfere.

What followed next was the Lepton Epoch, which occurred from one second to three minutes after the Big Bang in what was a still very elastic form of time. Lepton figured out how to sweep up most of the hadrons and anti-hadrons and balanced the books by annihilation of pairs of them.

At the end of the Hadron Epoch, leptons, such as electrons, and anti-leptons, such as positrons, dominated the mass of the Universe.

Lepton was pleased, thinking this would allow him to break free from the immutable timeline, but didn't realise that he had inadvertently created light. The newly dominant electrons and positrons collided creating new energy in the form of photons. Lepton had switched on a visible universe, without intending to.

Light - An unintended consequence.

Something else blew my mind. Since Lepton's discovery of Light, he also acquired another power. He could skate in either direction along the timeline.

"I never go back to the point before I gave my gift," he explained to me, "' I don't want to lose it and then not be able to provide it again."

But Lepton could be a scout for the rest of us about the future. He could slip forward but then slide backward with his report of what happened. He told me that there were a few others with similar powers. It is because of this that we could devise our plan around the beach fire.

We all knew that because of Lepton we had seen the wave of space surf crashing down and it made it more manageable to assimilate.

This is the point where creation scientists are convinced that stars cannot form spontaneously. And despite claims to the contrary, star formation seems to be nothing more than a secular attempt to explain the universe without invoking God.

The Bible's Genesis runs: *'Let there be lights in the expanse of the heavens to separate the day from the night. And let the lights be for signs and for seasons, and for days and years, and let there be lights in the expanse of the heavens to give light upon the Earth. And it was so.... And there was evening and there was morning, the fourth day.'*

Now we have secular 21st Century science vs Moses (who is the traditional author of Genesis in the 5th Century BC).

No explanations in Genesis. More a case of blind faith.

Now that was a big bump in logic to traverse but let us move onward.

The Nucleosynthesis Epoch, which supposedly lasted from three minutes to twenty minutes after the Big Bang showed the temperature of the universe falling to around one billion degrees Celsius (Bong) at which point atomic nuclei could begin to form as protons and neutrons; and combine through nuclear fusion to form the nuclei of simple chemical elements such as hydrogen, helium and lithium.

Watch out for H to He.

After around twenty minutes, the temperature and density of the universe had fallen to the point where such nuclear fusion could not continue. But we are still into Miracle territory.

Unlike Lepton, I was still reeling from this immensely fast activity and the intensity of the physical reactions. I had no idea that everything would soon slow down for billions of years.

I'd like to run an audit on those time suppositions to see if things could be shown to unfold in a more plausible way.

Take Population I, II, and III stars. Population I are the metal-rich stars (like the sun), then Population II are the metal-poor globular clusters like the centre of the Milky Way.

Now - here's the thing - Population III stars are allegedly supermassive, luminous and hot with no metals. Except that Population III stars are undetected. They are inferred - like they are from another dimension.

That's where we go back to Lepton. These Population III stars also get referred to as Dark Matter. That will increase in significance as we go along further. For now, let's just say it is where the dragons live.

It raises the question about whether the scientists are observing it all from the correct frame of reference / right room to devise their conclusions? Did Lepton only switch on one form of light? Maybe there are others that would allow us to see the other 85% of the matter in the universe?

After Lepton's Intervention which caused the Universe to become visible, the longer Photon Epoch was next, starting from three minutes and ending around 240,000 years after the Big Bang. During this long period of gradual cooling in temperature, the Universe filled with plasma - a hot, opaque soup of atomic nuclei and electrons.

Most of the leptons and anti-leptons had annihilated each other at the end of Lepton's Epoch, so that the energy of the Universe was dominated by photons, which continued to interact frequently with charged protons, electrons and nuclei.

The Recombination and Recoupling Epoch followed, from 240,000 to 300,000 years after the Big Bang; during which the temperature of the universe fell to around 6,000 degrees Celsius, which is around the same as the surface of the Sun.

This is where we get to something more understandable, and I'll believe the human numbers from this point, after which the convenience of reverse engineered assumptions becomes less important.

The density of the universe continued to fall as ionised hydrogen and helium atoms captured electrons and neutralised their electric charge. With the electrons now bound to atoms, the Universe finally became transparent to light, making this the earliest epoch observable today.

And now, the dark room used by science believers was suddenly bestowed with visibility. There was a comfortable frame of reference to explain many things after this point.

It was similarly convenient for science that the earlier part from zero to 300,000 years was all in complete darkness. By the end of this epoch, the known matter in the Universe consisted of about 75% hydrogen and 25% helium, and minute traces of helium.

There, I said Hydrogen to Helium was coming.

Come into my world

Come in, come in
Come into my world I've got to show
Show, show you
Come into my bed
I've got to know
Know, know you

I have dreams of Orca whales and owls
But I wake up in fear
You will never be my...
You will never be my fool
Will never be my fool

Regina Spektor

Fireside

It is unusual for Watchers to get together. We have other ways to communicate, so the physical manifestation of several of us together, such as in Point Reyes, is an exception.

One problem for us is to operate at Earth's speed. We can get close to it, but because we are used to striding through millennia, the small matter of a minute or a second can be troublesome. It's why we are more usually seen alone.

Fortunately, humans are not that observant. If we appear in the right clothes, the tell-tale signs we are Watchers become less apparent. An occasional blur or glitch when our timing goes adrift, or that strange moment when a human thinks she has seen one of us but then looks again and there is no one there.

Put several of us together on the beach and it is a different matter. We can all sync with one another, so any temporal drift is minimised as we self-correct from each other's vibes.

Limantour knew this as she leaned towards us. She was tending a kamado barbecue.

"So, will you support Tomales and me for this

Intervention? When we try to turn this situation around?"

I was taken aback. Being asked to be part of an Intervention is a big deal. There are other beings, the Wakeners, who are better placed for this task. And even for them it doesn't always end well.

Darnell - I'll tell you about him later - suffice to say he was really a Watcher who stepped too far, but also the Wakeners Leonardo and Galileo. They took something that was dormant in the culture of Earth and surfaced it, to either a kind of apathy or a violent dispute.

Leonardo's fortunes were mixed. Alongside his brilliance, he linked to a secret society known as the Priory of Sion, which started in 1099 and includes illustrious Grand Masters such as Isaac Newton.

The Priory of Sion is devoted to restoring the Merovingian dynasty (Mary Magdalene's bloodline), which ruled the Franks from 457 to 751, on the thrones of France and the rest of Europe. They are said to have created the Knights Templar as its military arm and financial branch. The Catholic Church tried to kill off Mary Magdalene's sacred royal bloodline (sometimes referred to as the Holy Grail) and their supposed guardians, the Cathars and the Templars, for popes to hold the Episcopal throne through the apostolic succession without fear of it ever being usurped by an antipope from the hereditary succession of Mary Magdalene.

So, for now, I'll use Galileo as the example. Galileo's championing of Copernican heliocentrism (Earth rotating daily and revolving around the sun) met with opposition from within the Catholic Church and from some astronomers. The Roman Inquisition investigated the matter in 1615, and concluded that heliocentrism was foolish, absurd, and heretical since it contradicted Holy Scripture. We saw a great scientist trying to give gifts to the world but being stamped upon by another belief system. Might commands over what is Right.

While I was thinking, we Watchers were running a back-channel of communication. It is faster than talking and can be used for difficult decisions.

Fireside support for Tomales and Limantour was forming. We would intervene to save the Earth. I had a feeling it wouldn't end there.

Early Universe

I had hung around in the early universe. It's where I first met Darnell. After all, it was all new. We didn't expect it to last for 370,000 years, so we both used judicious linked fast-forwarding during our combined process of inspection.

To begin with, it was still all kinds of subatomic particles re-balancing. Matter and anti-matter, against a background of persistent cosmic neutrinos. Then we get to where the opaque plasma cleared because of cooling, plus Lepton's considerate addition of photonic light.

Darnell was hooked by what Lepton had achieved, even if it was accidental. Darnell decided he wanted to leave a similar mark, despite being a Watcher.

I already mentioned Hydrogen and Helium. They were the fuel needed to fire up the first stars, but the clouds of hydrogen only collapsed slowly to form stars and galaxies, so there were no alternative sources of light. Those decoupled photons filled the universe with a brilliant pale orange glow at first, gradually red shifting to non-visible wavelengths after about 3 million years. One could say it was the cosmic Dark Ages.

I could see that Darnell was going out of his mind. It was a combination of the boredom of having to deal with such long periods of nothing much happening followed by short bursts of frantic activity. Both Darnell and I used our ability our fast-forward through time, but it still took a seemingly long time to get to the next interesting occurrence.

Fast forward then, to when the earliest generations of stars and galaxies formed and large structures gradually emerge, drawn to the foam-like dark matter filaments which had already begun to weave together throughout the universe.

The dark matter filaments were the ones the star gods used for travel.

Those early stars were huge, around 100 to 300 times the size of the Sun, but they sputtered out quickly, exploding as highly energetic unstable supernovae after mere millions of years.

Through all of this, we Watchers sat on the outside, literally watching the Universe like a very long cosmic documentary.

We eventually got to a billion years from the start and the universe took on its recognisable shape. The Dark Ages of galaxy clusters, superclusters, dwarf galaxies and quasars led to the period of deionization and the transitioning of the entire universe into its recognisable form.

This is where we really needed the three arrows fast-forward button to jump over the next eleven billion years.

The thin disk of Earth's galaxy formed at about 5 billion years from zero and the Solar System formed at about 9.2

billion years, with the earliest traces of life on Earth emerging by about 10.3 billion years.

That is a long time to watch and to wait. I guess that is how we acquired the name - Watchers.

Except Darnell wanted more. He was first plotting and then looking for his chance.

The thinning of matter over time reduced the ability of gravity to decelerate the expansion of the universe. In contrast, dark energy is a constant factor tending to accelerate the expansion of the universe. The universe's expansion passed an inflection point about five or six billion years ago, when the universe entered the modern 'dark-energy-dominated era' where the universe's expansion is now accelerating rather than decelerating.

Right now, human scientists say they understand the universe well, but I see gaps in their knowledge. Metaverses like the ones that we Watchers can inhabit are still seen as the stuff of comic books and cartoons. And even worse, jumped-up billionaire businessmen are trying to commercialise their own shoddy form of metaverse.

One thing is certain. The current Stelliferous Era will end when stars are no longer being born, and any continued expansion of the universe will mean that the observable universe will become limited to local galaxies.

Darnell and I could see and hear scientists explaining the Big Bang and not even mention the other theories. Edwin Hubble may have spotted the redshift of an expanding universe, but there could be so many other explanations. Similarly, the lightest elements of hydrogen, helium and lithium were rising to the top, much like the way small pieces fall to the bottom in a cereal box- the path of least resistance.

As for that background temperature of 2.75 Celsius, it could be worked backwards into the proof calculations.

Add in clashing 'branes of space and you could have whole different theories available, but humans have insufficient mathematics to express them.

For example, the black hole bounce-back theory could create a whole different science system in a different universe - another different darkened room.

Or there is the vortex theory of superfluid space-time, with space and time flowing with zero friction.

Darnell had asked what this could all mean. He asked me several times, because he knew I had some kind of special interaction with gravity.

Darnell's thought was that humanity sought its comfortable answer and, in doing so, has limited its outer range of thinking. The scientific explanation used is still mumbo-jumbo to most people, but plausible enough for well-meaning scientists to buy into it.

The Great Deception

Moon's teeth marks

And the moon's teeth marks are on the sky
Like a tarp thrown all over this
And the broken umbrellas like dead birds
And the steam comes out of the grill like
The whole goddamned town is ready to blow.

And the bricks are all scarred with jailhouse tattoos
And everyone is behaving like dogs.
And the horses are coming down Violin Road
And Dutch is dead on his feet
And all the rooms they smell like diesel
And you take on the dreams of the ones who have slept
here.

And I'm lost in the window
And I hide on the stairway
And I hang in the curtain
And I sleep in your hat.
And no one brings anything
Small into a bar around here.

Dark forces

We'd been at the fireside for well over an hour. This was a long and comforting time to spend in the presence of other Watchers. Remember, we Watchers are not supposed have prāṇa - that 'life force' thing - so I was slightly surprised that I felt anything at all.

Limantour spoke again, "We'd have to avoid any of the dark forces. Just because Lepton showed us Light doesn't mean that there are no problems waiting for us."

Limantour was referring to the darkness which dominated the universe. Only 20% of it was matter and the rest was still, well, undefined. Another literally darkened room.

Drake spoke up. "Can we be sure of Lepton's report? I mean, he might try anything to be back on the inside with all of us?"

Tomales spoke. "No, Lepton has gone beyond us all. Just like we are beyond all the humans. We can envisage alternate realities, but Lepton is already in one of them."

Abbott spoke forcefully, "I can discuss this with my other associates: Bishop and Cardinal. They will also be certain to have a source for the knowledge-shards."

Knowledge shards - the elements for new knowledge which could be positioned into humanity's awareness to speed up certain discoveries.

"But if the k-shards are a bundle, we won't know exactly what we are sending towards Earth. How can we say that the other components included are all benign?" I asked.

Limantour answered, "Yes. I wondered about that too. We need to be sure that the k-shards can't do anything drastic."

"It's cool," answered Abbott. He was clutching a small branch, which he dropped onto the fire, "The k-shard bundle we use will have the magnetite as its pinnacle discovery; everything else will be contained in a knowledge triangle underneath it. Think of the magnetite as the transcendent growth need, and the other items below it as the deficiency needs."

"Hah," said Drake, "Like Maslow?"

"Kinda," answered Abbott, "Think of the magnetite use as the outer boundary of what can be achieved in this bundle of k-shards."

"So, we are not introducing any unwanted payload?" asked Tomales.

"No," answered Abbott. I had an uneasy feeling about just how quickly he had replied. I think Tomales did as well.

"Okay, well, that's settled," said Limantour. "We have a plan for intervention. We'll deflect Hubble Four by one degree and simultaneously rain some new relevant knowledge toward Earth. The humans will piece it together. Magnetite to supply clean, almost free power and be used to build tiny propulsion units capable of interstellar transportation."

Tomales, "Yes, they should be able to see that magnetite enables whole new inexpensive power sources coupled with an end to pollution. An ability to reverse climate catastrophe."

Limantour added, "This could be a great Intervention."

Watchers

I'll have to explain myself as a Watcher. I'm not some kind of superhero with special strength and flying powers. Some might attempt to classify me as an angel, or as a super-watchful guardian. Those people are trying to define me and thus to take control of my label.

It doesn't work like that. I'm outside of those classifications, my personal metaverse is altogether more permeable. Whether Aramaic, Theodotian, Greek, from the Book of Daniel or the Books of Enoch, humankind wants it to become all about classification.

None of these religion-like attempts are even close and yet, menacingly, they extort control over the belief system using stories of fallen angels, mass defections and even a race of hybrids which mankind called Nephilim and who are referenced in many versions of Numbers 13:33.

Now I can say that Erwin Schrödinger got close to understanding the Watchers. He defended what scientists dismiss as metaphysics — that realm of knowledge that lies beyond the current scientific tools and modes of truth-extraction, which always reveals more about the limitations of the human tools than about the limits of nature's truths.

Schrödinger wrote:

'It is relatively easy to sweep away the whole of metaphysics, as Kant did. The slightest puff in its direction blows it away, and what was needed was not so much a powerful pair of lungs to provide the blast, as a powerful dose of courage to turn it against so timelessly venerable a house of cards.

'But you must not think that what has then been achieved is the actual elimination of metaphysics from the empirical content of human knowledge.

'In fact, if we cut out all metaphysics, it will be found to be vastly more difficult, indeed probably quite impossible, to give any intelligible account of even the most circumscribed area of specialisation within any specialised science you please.'

Even as Schrödinger made his reality-reconfiguring contributions to science and its search for fundamental truth, he never relinquished his passionate curiosity about philosophy and the ongoing questions of meaning that kernel every truth in the flesh of consciousness.

Schrödinger was as drawn to Spinoza and Schopenhauer as he was to the ancient Eastern traditions, and especially in their untrammelled common ground of believing that everything has a mind.

As a Watcher, I've progressively discovered others like me. I mentioned Darnell, who stood out as one who was attempting to change things. And that Lepton is not Lekton (to those that know); Lekton was an altogether different and darker being, and I only ran into him much later.

Darrell really wanted to copy the process of Lepton, to accelerate a discovery and somehow escape the tedium he felt he experienced as a Watcher. Darnell also inhabits a different realm now and, like Lepton, can move both ways along the time axis.

As Watchers we are not supposed to change anything in case it trips off parallel realities but more especially because of unintended consequences.

You know the kind of thing. The building correction at Pisa that didn't work, leading to an unintended consequence that the Leaning Tower became a tourist attraction. Introducing 100 non-native starlings into Central Park, because they were like the birds that Shakespeare saw. Now there's 60 million of them across the USA. I could go on, but it is best to remember when we try to pick out anything by itself, we find it hitched to everything else in the universe.

Second Level thinking

I've already mentioned the opposing questions to a few scientific facts. The Big Bang's implausibly packed first second of time. The immense heat of the apple-sized crushed universe. So-called Population III stars.

Roll into second order thinking. Ask "And then what?"

Watchers learn that first-level thinking is simplistic and superficial, and just about everyone can do it. All the first-level thinker needs is an opinion about the future, as in 'The outlook for the company is favourable, meaning the stock will go up.' It is often espoused by pundits and the people propping up a corner of a bar-room.

First-order thinking is fast, easy and some could say lazy. It happens when we look for something that only solves the immediate problem without considering the consequences. For example, think of this as 'I'm hungry, so let's eat a chocolate bar.'

Second-order thinking is more deliberate. Watchers think in terms of interactions and time, understanding that despite intentions, the interventions often cause harm. Second order thinkers ask themselves the question

'And then what?' This means thinking about the consequences of repeatedly eating a chocolate bar when you are hungry and using that to inform your decision. If you do this, you're more likely to eat something healthy.

The road to out-thinking people can't come from first-order thinking. It must come from second-order thinking and beyond. Seeing things that other people can't see.

It raises a question about proof. A simple example would be the very ley lines where we meet around the fire.

Some might contest the validity of ley lines. It would be another way of toppling some scientific investigations. It doesn't fit into the right box, so the theories are mocked and dashed with subtle passive-aggressive asides.

"Ley lines? What've you been smoking, at Glastonbury/Coachella?" and so it runs.

It suits the darker forces to remain in stealth. To reject nascent discoveries. It could become a problem for any new knowledge shards installed by Watchers or Wakeners. Would Earth-science simply repel all attempts at knowledge that doesn't fit its self-absorbed framework, or would humankind, like with Leonardo, take hundreds of years to realise the truths in what was being described?

I realised that what Limantour and Tomales were proposing would require more than a gentle intervention to be successful. It would probably need major event to act as a catalyst.

Tomales continued, "We will use the Swiss Research Lab CERN with its hadron collider to produce the needed accelerant for our deeds. It, coincidentally, is also sited on a well-known ley line."

Limantour added, "To emphasise its significance, the entrance to CERN already has a colossal statue of the Hindu Goddess of destruction 'Kali', right in front of its reception."

We all smiled. Limantour could be obsessive about symbolism.

Tomales continued, "Now we could also locate a few other equivalent labs. The Brookhaven Lab in New York also sits on ley lines and has a Hadron Collider. And similarly there's a lab in Alaska and another in Bodø, Norway. Even a lab north of Moscow, run by the Moscow University."

"Are you about to start a nuclear war?" asked Drake. "There is only so much you can do with a handful of particle accelerators."

"Fear in a handful of dust?" asked Tomales.

"Highly accelerated dust!" answered Drake.

Limantour smiled, "We need to bypass general science and get directly to the smart people who work with properties like strangeness and charm. That way, we can keep things moving along. A gift of new theoretical physics, unlocking secrets of gluons and providing ways to harness hypercharges."

Limantour continued, "This could show them how to use the intrinsic power of magnetite to create small yet impressively powerful motors. They don't use fuel because of an entirely safe electromagnetic interaction. In sensible hands, this is a massive game-changer."

An annoying thing about humans is they have self-interest at the front of their cerebral cortex. Even by simultaneously planting k-shards around the Earth, it would still take a miracle for someone to interpret their findings and make the link to magnetite. Otherwise, they could all be competing to listen to different tunes on the radio

What happened to Darnell

Limantour continued to tend the barbecue, which looked like a big green egg. Wafts of delicious cooking were blowing through the wind. This was a good day to be operating at Earth's speed, but I could sense that Limantour and Tomales must really want something if they were going to this much trouble.

"Farallon?" said Limantour; she was looking at me.

This was the first time she'd called me by name in maybe a millennium. I waited for the next line. I could sense it would be a request.

"We'd like you to do something, Farallon," says Limantour. She was casually plating the barbecued food.

"It'd be like something that Darnell did once before," adds Tomales.

"But we all know what happened to Darnell," I say, "After all, he was on the same timeline as the rest of the Watchers."

"Yes," says Tomales, "But Darnell became enthused with

an idea about ways to accelerate the process of Earth's creation and, more importantly, how to introduce sentient beings. Now we are trying to save that same Earth from extinction."

I spoke, "Remember that the period from the beginning to the formation of Earth? All 8.3 billion years of it? That's 5.4 billion years in the past. Darnell didn't take to it well."

I thought to myself; even at a speedy fast-forward rate, it had been an immense amount of time to traverse. Take a year as 31.5 million seconds. Forwarding at the rate of a year every second, it still would still take around 264 years to get from the beginning of the Universe to the beginning of the Earth. And that's if you skip the bits where the Andromeda Galaxy forms, or the Milky Way, or even Alpha Centauri is first observable.

Fortunately, we could bypass such constraints to move through time even faster.

Drake spoke, "Let's face it, we all knew that Darnell wasn't prepared to sit out billennia and that is why he started to obsess over ways to accelerate evolution."

Abbott interjected, "We have to remember that the original Earth wasn't that pretty, nor sweet smelling either."

"No, it was disgusting," added Limantour, "Today, humans take for granted that they live among diverse communities of animals that feed on each other. Earth's ecosystems are structured by feeding relationships like killer whales eating seals, which eat squid, which feed on krill. These and other animals require oxygen to extract energy from their food. But that's not how life on Earth used to be."

Drake added, "Darnell knew Earth needed adjustments and wanted to boost the oxygen content and reduce the amount of methane."

Abbott continued, "The earliest life forms we know of were microbes - microscopic organisms that left signs of their presence in rocks about 3.7 billion years old. Humans can look backwards through time to see these signals of a type of carbon molecule that is produced by living things. Evidence of microbes was also preserved in the hard sticky mats known as stromatolites that they made and which date to 3.5 billion years ago."

Drake added, "Eventually, some microbes began a remarkable transformation. One that is in part down to Lepton's inadvertent release of photons."

Drake continued, "These microbes became Earth's first photo-synthesizers, making food using water and the Sun's energy, and releasing oxygen as a result. This catalysed a sudden, dramatic rise in oxygen, making the environment less hospitable for other microbes that could not tolerate oxygen."

Abbott interrupted, "It also stiffened Darnell's resolve to expedite more oxygen for Earth."

He continued, "Today, scientists can see the evidence for this in Earth's seafloor rocks. With oxygen around, iron gets oxidised and removed. Rocks dating before Darnell's event are striped with bands of iron. Rocks dating after the transformation do not have iron bands, showing that oxygen was now in the picture. We are still talking about 2.4 billion years ago."

Drake continued, "Darnell had plenty of time to think

about what he would do. He was convinced that adding more oxygen to the Earth, to counteract the effects of the methane, would bring forward the next evolutionary phase by perhaps a couple of billion years."

Now Limantour spoke up whilst handing me a plate of barbecued deliciousness, "Darnell also noticed that profound innovations were occurring. Microbes can process lots of chemicals, but they did not have the specialised cells needed for complex bodies."

I sensed they were all quietly ganging up on me. Pushing me toward a corner.

Tomales spoke, "Darnell noticed that something revolutionary was happening as microbes began living inside other microbes, functioning as organelles for them. Mitochondria, the organelles that process food into energy, developed from these mutually beneficial relationships. For the first time, DNA became packaged in nuclei. The new complex cells - eukaryotic cells - incorporated parts playing specialised roles that supported the whole cell."

Limantour continued, "Darnell was looking for an early organism that could rapidly multiply and additionally produce large quantities of oxygen."

Now Tomales and I knew I was being overwhelmed, "Even today, school children on Earth are taught about the different parts of the single cell organism known as Amoeba, but the significance of its component parts maybe isn't emphasised enough."

Tomales continued, "This type of cell surrounds and engulfs its food and has a nucleus to carry DNA and a vacuole to regulate water ingestion. Now, groups of these cells began living together because certain benefits could be obtained. Groups of cells might feed more efficiently or gain protection from simply being bigger."

I could see what they were doing. The equivalent of 'get him saying Yes'. They would produce a string of incontestable facts in a row. Ones that it was easy for me to agree with. Then they would slip in the trick fact.

Tomales was still talking, "Darnell began to look beyond single cells towards slightly more complex organisms, and was always on the lookout for something small, that multiplied quickly and created exceptional quantities of oxygen."

I was trying to concentrate on something else. I realised I could slow down their fast forward of the facts, so I wouldn't miss the treats of the last 800 million years as Earth's inhabitants changed from resource-devouring sponges into politicians.

Tomales was on roll, and added, "The combined clusters of specialised, cooperating cells eventually became the first animals, which DNA evidence suggests evolved around 800 million years ago. Sponges were among the earliest animals. While chemical compounds from sponges are preserved in rocks as old as 700 million years, molecular evidence points to sponges developing even earlier."

Tomales and Limantour were still operating as a tag team, and now Limantour took over, "Oxygen levels in the ocean were still low compared to today, but sponges are able to tolerate conditions of low oxygen."

Then Drake piped up, "The sponges were a disappointment to Darnell because, like other animals, they required oxygen to metabolize, but they need little because they were not very active. They feed while sitting still by extracting food particles from water that is pumped through their bodies by specific cells. The simple body plan of a sponge comprises layers of cells around water-filled cavities, supported by hard skeletal parts. The evolution of ever more complex and diverse body plans would eventually lead to distinct groups of animals."

"This is all wrong," Darnell had said. "Earth can't just be inhabited by idle sponges." He set about looking at the genetics of the sponges.

I thought, "Or can it?"

Drake added, "Darnell realised that assembly instructions for the body plan are in a sponge's genes. Some genes act like orchestra conductors, controlling the expression of many other genes at specific places and times to correctly assemble the components. While they were not played out immediately, there is evidence that parts of instructions for complex bodies were present even in the earliest animals."

I realised that Darnell's supposition was to find something to kick evolution over the edge.

Tomales continued, "Darnell knew it was a slow process. Another 220 million years passed, and we reached the Ediacaran Period, some 580 million years ago. It is easier to count backwards now, instead of time elapsed, saying how long-ago various events occurred. Now at 1 second per year, that's only around seven years, although I'm guessing Darnell did all of his work in about half of that time."

She added, "No longer did we find just sponges, but also varied seafloor creatures - with bodies shaped like fronds, ribbons, and even quilts which lived alongside sponges for 80 million years. By the end of the Ediacaran, oxygen levels rose, approaching levels sufficient to sustain oxygen-based life."

Limantour took over again, "The early sponges may actually have helped boost oxygen by eating bacteria, removing them from the decomposition process. Darnell's idea was to engineer a major environmental change by boosting the oxygen balance on Earth. It was through the introduction of several handfuls of trilobites. These were armoured creatures he identified which could burrow along the seabed, aerating the sediment. Being small scale, they multiplied rapidly, and it led to the Cambrian explosion of new life forms."

I recollected. Some 541-485 million years ago we didn't just get the burrowing trilobites. We also got hard body parts like shells and spines which allowed animals to engineer their environments more drastically, such as digging burrows. This was because the oxygen rich Earth could now provide fuel for these new and more active animals, with defined heads and tails for directional movement to chase prey.

We were witnessing Darnell's trilobites leading to the inadvertent introduction of insects too.

As Darnell's trilobites transitioned to crustaceans, the first land-bound insects emerged. Then, about 400 million years ago in the Devonian period one lineage of insects evolved flight, the first animals to do so.

The trilobites became extinct and were replaced with molluscs, arthropods, and annelids. Now we had diversity and the emergence of food chains (well food webs, at least).

Darnell accelerated the introduction of lifeforms to Earth through the much greater generation of oxygen.

But here's the thing. The insects didn't know when to stop. They proliferated, but also grew bigger. Many of these insects were the size of small mammals, and it was only their lack of body structure that stopped them from growing even larger. It is why so many humans today have an instinctive fear of crawly things. These early insects could bring down large mammals - instinctively attacking their neck and injecting toxins. It was the playing out of the law of unintended consequences, in this case Darnell's consequences.

Some might say it was fortunate that global climate conditions changed several times during the history of Earth, and along with it the diversity of insects. Winged insects underwent a major expansion in the Carboniferous (356 to 299 million years ago) while insects that go through different life stages with metamorphosis underwent another major expansion in the Permian (299 to 252 million years ago).

Darnell had rolled the evolutionary dice with a few handfuls of trilobites. He'd accelerated oxygen creation on Earth, brought through the development of insects and seen the rapid development of many now extinct Earth species.

He'd also spent a considerable time planning it, although I'm dubious whether he could have foreseen the evolution from trilobite to crustacean to the burgeoning classes of insect.

None of us are clear how Darnell, like Lepton, ceased being a Watcher and seemed to acquire some new powers after this Intervention. But he moved to the same plane as Lepton and could skitter along the planetary timeline.

The Great Dying

I suspected I was being asked to do something similar to Darnell, by Limantour, but without the millennia of thought ahead of the deed. If Darnell had introduced trilobites, and they had led to oxygen creation to fuel the rise in life, then it was a pretty cool Intervention.

Let's face it, Darnell's Intervention ended when most insects had developed, but many early groups became extinct during the mass extinction event at the Permian and Triassic boundary. It was the largest extinction event in the history of the Earth, often referred to as The Great Dying and occurred around 252 million years ago.

There were two concurrent events. An asteroid hit the Earth; there is even evidence in the form of fullerenes containing noble gases in the form of 3He and 36Ar atoms -- Helium and Argon isotopes that are more common in space than on Earth.

It was at the same time as huge volcanic eruptions in Siberia created immense choking dust in the atmosphere.

World geography was also changing. Plate tectonics pushed the continents together to form the super-continent Pangea and the super-ocean Panthalassa.

Weather patterns and ocean currents shifted, many coastlines and their shallow marine ecosystems vanished, sea levels dropped. Do all of that to the Earth and inevitably life forms take a tumble.

This Great Dying formed the boundary between the Permian and Triassic geologic periods, as well as between the Palaeozoic and Mesozoic eras, approximately 252 million years ago.

It was the Earth's most severe known extinction event, with the extinction of 57% of biological families, 83% of genera, 81% of marine species and 70% of terrestrial vertebrate species. It was the largest known mass extinction of insects.

It pulled the curtain around what Darnell had done, and left no evidence of the wilder excesses, except for a latent genetic instinctive fear in humans of insects and arachnids.

There were three distinct pulses of extinction. The causes of extinction were elevated temperatures and widespread oceanic anoxia and acidification due to the large amounts of carbon dioxide that were emitted by the massive eruption of Siberian volcanoes.

Then there was the burning of hydrocarbon deposits, including oil and coal, by these volcanoes and emissions of methane by methanogenic microorganisms contributing to the extinction. The planet was coated with dust, so there was no light, which limited oxygen production and created and a toxic surface. No wonder little could survive. But what did survive were some of the most robust life forms.

The survivors of these terrible events evolved in the

Triassic (252 to 201 million years ago) to what are essentially the modern insect orders that persist to this day. Most modern insect families appeared in the Jurassic (201 to 145 million years ago). No wonder humankind thinks the ant will survive everything.

In an important example of co-evolution, several highly successful insect groups — especially the Hymenoptera (wasps, bees and ants) and Lepidoptera (butterflies) as well as many types of Diptera (flies) and Coleoptera (beetles) — evolved in conjunction with flowering plants during the Cretaceous (145 to 66 million years ago).

And so it goes on; many modern insect genera developed during the Cenozoic that began about 66 million years ago; insects from this period frequently became preserved in amber, often in perfect condition. Such specimens are easily compared with modern species, and most of them are recognisable as part of the same species.

Out of Space - Prodigy

I'll take your brains to another dimension

*I'm gon' send him to outer space
To find another race*

*I'll take your brains to another dimension
Pay close attention*

Cedric Miller / Keith Thornton / Lee Perry / Maurice
Smith / Max Romeo / Trevor Randolph

Cherry wood chips and a handful of pecans

We'd all eaten by this time; Limantour had used cherry wood chips and a handful of pecans to slow cook the short ribs. She'd added butter and bourbon and glazed it all with garlic, ginger, soy, maple syrup and cider vinegar. Then served it with leek. It was mind-blowing, but Limantour knew good ideas were best consumed with the best food.

"So, we'll be asking for your help?"

I looked around the circle. They knew my special skills would help.

    A) To Deflect the Hubble Four by one degree.

    B) To Set off a gravity ripple which would bring humankind a shower of knowledge-shards.

"Okay, if I help you, how do I know I won't end up like Darnell?"

Tomales answered, "We don't know that, but think of it. The ability to pass both ways along the timeline. At least to the point at which you introduced your Intervention."

"That's around now. But I can' go back further?"

"Yes, but you can't do that at present," answered Drake. "This is all about gain."

"Gain for you, and gain for Earth," said Tomales.

"We thought long and hard about a candidate for this," said Limantour. "It had to be you."

I could see they had me surrounded.

I said we Watchers didn't have superpowers. That's correct in the conventional sense. We can't fly or throw cars around. But we've all got some special features. Mine is to bend gravity.

I don't know why. I can see the forces of gravity and can manipulate them very precisely.

Not strongly, but enough for it to be interesting. For example, I cannot make everyone heavier or lighter, neither can I fly, but I could manipulate gravity as a weak force, with surprisingly big effects. I never use the power. It seems to me to be more trouble than it is worth.

Take it to the limit

I looked toward Drake. He was agitated.

"We need to move; we've been in this place nearing the maximus."

The maximus was the longest time we Watchers could stay assembled in one spot. We all knew it as a quarter revolution of the Earth, but we used 5 hours to provide a safety margin. Failing that, we'd be dispersed and thrown forward to random locations. It wasn't a showstopper, but reminded us all that we were not in control.

"We'll need to continue this somewhere else," said Limantour. I looked along the beach. 'Leave no trace' was an understatement. The barbecue and its trappings had already been flipped into another chaotic metaverse by Limantour. I could envisage some unsuspecting human finding it at the back of piles of rubbish in their yard.

"Tread lightly upon the Earth," said Tomales, smiling towards me. An obvious cliche. I could tell they thought they had me ensnared.

"Where then?" I asked.

"We'll stay with the ley lines but find another point of maximum convergence."

"Le Mont-Saint-Michel," said Limantour, "In France,"

We all knew it. A tidal island and mainland commune in Normandy. The commune's position—on an island just a few hundred metres from land—once made it accessible at low tide to the many pilgrims to its abbey, but defensible. An incoming tide stranded, drove off, or drowned would-be assailants. Nowadays, I realised that outside of tourist hours it was an ideally isolated place. The abbey had been used regularly as a prison during the Ancien Régime exactly because of its isolation.

But we must go back further.

The Mont occupied dry land in prehistoric times. As sea levels rose, erosion reshaped the coastal landscape, and several outcrops of granite emerged in the bay, having resisted the wear and tear of the ocean better than the surrounding rocks. Mont-Saint-Michel consists of granite solidified from molten magma about 525 million years ago, during the Cambrian period.

We each had our different ways to transport ourselves to the new meeting point, and I just hoped our varied routes would not be detected by any of the modern-day Earth dwellers. I knew that much of our science was still in another dimension from that discovered by mankind. They were still in their darkened room.

Now we were sitting inside the Abbey, or maybe still outside? The lights played tricks here and there were many concealed courtyards, such that it becomes difficult to know what is inside and outside. The Benedictine monks knew how to play tricks, even from the 8th Century.

"Something I don't understand," I began, "Is how we

know what bundle of knowledge shards to return to Earth?"

"Don't worry," said Tomales, "Darnell has explained it to Abbott; He has researched the exact combination. Your role, Farallon, is to create a gravity wave which can trigger the release of the shards. Think of it as a signal."

This made more sense to me. I could use my ability to create gravity waves for both purposes. First, to disturb the Hubble Four by one degree; and second, to send a gravity wave which could be received by distant galaxies and would permit them to send a targeted wave towards Earth. A wave which could flip knowledge from another dimension into the Universe.

"But what form do the k-shards take?" I asked.

"They will look like a metallic rain which will fall upon Earth," explained Tomales, "But once they are discovered and disturbed by humans, they will be able to use the knowledge contained within. It will accelerate their comprehension of certain key matters."

"You are sure that this is pure? Knowledge for good intentions?" asked Drake.

"Certainly," answered Abbott, "And I have asked the same questions of Darnell."

I could still feel misgivings when Abbott spoke, but this break from the ennui of a Watcher was overshadowed by the excitement of the moment.

And now, here we all were sitting in the middle of a medieval monastery on a powerful ley line plotting to execute an Intervention.

PART TWO

To the Ghosts Who Write History Books

To them ghosts that write history books
To them ghosts that write songs
Everyone asks would you write one about me
To them ghosts in the train yard
All them ghosts in my drink
Your money's no good here just write one about me

And when you go, where the winds are strong
When you go where flowers bend
Please take along all the best of my luck
and come back unchanged
Your demons all tamed
Your flowers uncut

And when you go where the winds are strong
Where soldiers carve their stones
Please take along all the best of my luck
and come back unchanged
Your demons all tamed
Your flowers uncut

Benjamin Knox Miller / Jeffrey Carl Prystowsky / Jocelyn
Jager Adams

Modified Newtonian Dynamics

I mentioned my ability to bend gravity. Not the coolest of effects, I admit. And it has a stigma attached.

It relates to dark matter, or the other 80 per cent of the universe. There's a human theory called MOND - "Modified Newtonian Dynamics" which suggests that darkmatter may actually not comprise any particles but could be attributed to the 'odd' behaviour of gravity.

Some human scientists claim that gravity does not fade away as quickly as current theories say it does. This 'stronger gravity' may be the dark matter holding together galaxies.

My clue: It is where the other dark rooms are hidden.

Further, this 'Cosmic Ghost' theory is an attempt to resolve three mysteries of modern cosmology, in one 'ghostly' presence.

Astrophysicists refer to the 'ghost condensate' in their revised modelling. They envisage it to produce a gravity to drive cosmic inflation in the Big Bang; and it may also account for the current rapid acceleration of the Universe, which has been attributed to unknowndark energy. The hypothesis that this ghost condensate could combine into particles of mass and thus could account for dark matter. I guess a few 'Bongs!' need to go with those last thoughts.

It reminds me of talk of Phlogiston by Johann Joachim Becher in the 1600s. It seems incredible that it was so long after Darnell's Intervention to give the Earth life-supporting quantities of oxygen.

According to Becher, substances that burned in air were said to be rich in phlogiston. That combustion soon ceased in an enclosed space was taken as clear-cut evidence that air had the capacity to absorb only a finite amount of phlogiston.

When air had become completely phlogisticated it would no longer serve to support combustion of any material, nor could phlogisticated air support life. Breathing was thought to take phlogiston out of the body. It was another science theory eventually debunked in the 1700s by the discovery of oxygen.

But back to the ghost condensate. Scientists are still using the current mathematical frame of reference and with it define 'Sterile Neutrinos' implying that dark matter is made of conveniently elusive particles.

Human science considers sterile neutrinos heavier than known neutrinos and may interact with other matter only through the force of gravity, making them impossible to detect. Sterile neutrinos could also be essential in the formation of stars and galaxies. Or it could all be hokum as human science toils in its lonely dark room.

To my mind, playing with gravity is toying with a serious and dark force always just eluding human vision. It's the dragon that follows me, always just on the corner of my eye. From Rene Descartes to Morpheus, humankind has always tried to look beyond its walls. For

Limantour's low-key sounding project, I was terrified that I was being asked to steal the fire from heaven.

So here I am, seated in the Benedictine abbey, surrounded by other Watchers. In our timeline we know Earth was once populated with small living creatures, survivors of an asteroid collision and a mysterious wipe-out of the Earth's climate.

I was about to engineer another possibly similar wipe.

"Think of the dinosaurs," said Abbott, "We've all experienced that. Evolution theory may be sketchy for them, although we've seen that dinosauromorphs were small animals, larger than insects but maybe only reaching the size of a house cat.

Limantour added, "The oldest dinosaurs were from Argentina, and they were around 231 million years old. There are several dinosaurs of this age found together, including the horse-sized meat-eater Herrerasaurus, the dog-sized meat-eater Eodromaeus (a distant relative of T. rex), and several dog-to-bear-sized cousins of the giant long-necked sauropods, including Panphagia and Eoraptor."

Abbott nodded, "The fact that so many dinosaurs, with different diets and sizes, lived at this time tells us that dinosaurs were already diversifying soon after they evolved from other reptiles."

Drake added, "But what you've just described are a grouping of dinosaurs any of which would terrify humans. But none of these dinosaurs were giants, and none were at the top of the food chain. Those species would come later, during the Jurassic Period."

Limantour continued, "Yes. 201 million years ago to around 145 million years ago is the time when the dinosaurs developed, roamed the Earth and were then wiped out."

Abbott added, "Every reptile and mammal had something else it could eat."

Limantour again, "Remember that by the beginning of the Jurassic, the supercontinent Pangaea had rifted into two landmasses: Laurasia to the north and Gondwana to the south. The climate of the Jurassic was warmer than the present, and there were no ice caps. Forests grew close to the poles, with large expanses of desert in the lower latitudes. The fauna transitioned to one dominated by dinosaurs alone."

Drake smiled, "The first birds appeared during the Jurassic. Other major events include the appearance of the earliest lizards and the evolution of therian/marsupial mammals. Crocodylomorphs made the transition from a terrestrial to an aquatic life. The oceans were inhabited by marine reptiles such as ichthyosaurs and plesiosaurs, while pterosaurs were the dominant flying vertebrates."

I was still thinking about what Abbott had said, 'Every reptile and mammal had something else it could eat.'

I remembered the collapse of the food chain ecosystem around 66 million years ago. We'd already seen a mass extinction during The Great Dying, and then we had another one. For the first 175 million years of their existence, dinosaurs took on a huge variety of forms as the environment changed and new species evolved that were suited to these new conditions. Dinosaurs that failed to adapt became extinct. But then 66 million years ago, over a relatively short time, the dinosaurs, except for birds, disappeared completely during the Cretaceous extinction.

This was caused by another 15-kilometre-wide asteroid impact, in Yucatán Peninsula in Mexico. A few minutes later and it would have hit the sea. Instead, the crash created the 150-kilometre-wide Chicxulub crater and threw huge amounts of debris into the air and caused massive tidal waves to wash over parts of the American continents.

Around three-quarters of Earth's animals, including dinosaurs, suddenly died. The asteroid hit at high velocity and effectively vaporised. It made a huge crater, devastating the immediate area. A huge blast wave and heat wave went out, and it threw vast amounts of material up into the atmosphere. It sent dust all around the world. It didn't completely block out the Sun, but it reduced the amount of light that reached the Earth's surface, impacting plant growth and, in turn, right the way up the food chain.

"Okay, so how will we do this, and when?" asked Abbott. He stared across at me. I noticed he was sitting in a shadowy corner and somehow his presence melted into the darkness.

Limantour stood, "Farallon has had time to think about this now, and I guess must have seen this request coming?"

I hadn't seen it coming, and I had no actual idea what to do. Cornered; that's what I felt. I could envisage a different perception if I said 'yes' and wondered if I would even be in the same dimension.

One thing for certain: I knew I'd be unable to continue as a Watcher.

"Don't you see?" asked Drake. "It's the whole point. We are Watchers until one day we are not. If we get involved - Intervene - then we become something else. I guess you, if successful, would be a Wakener."

"But what about if something goes wrong?" I asked.

Abbott answered, "Can it really be any more mundane that a life as a Watcher? Seeing 13.8 billion years of history unspool until Earth and then the Universe run into an end-state?"

Limantour and Tomales were both nodding.

"I need some time to think," I said, aware of how ridiculous this must sound. A Watcher asking for more time.

"Three days," spoke Abbott, "That should be long enough to weigh the options."

"I'll want to talk to a few people too," I said.

Limantour spoke again. "We'll be able to help you. Who would you like to speak to?"

"Two people first," I said, "Lepton and Darnell." Lepton because he'd done something agreed to be successful - i.e., Light, and Darnell because his intervention was more controversial.

"I can assist that," said Abbott.

"And then a third person," they all looked at me.

"Limantour. Alone," I looked across to her. She looked back, then nodded.

"Agreed, although if you speak to me alone the others will probably be able to share it via the back-channel we've created between us all."

Limantour looked around. I could tell that some of the others wanted to honour my privacy with Limantour. But not everyone.

"Okay, we'll worry about that when it happens," I said.

Three days. Three people. All of them Watchers. Two of them already Wakeners.

Ice, ice, baby

I must recognise us crossing a huge bookmark in time. It was when Earth's ice ages occurred. Some might call it climate change, but that understates its significance. Some people think of simply one ice age, and I suppose as a Watcher you'd be able to fast forward from 2.4 million years ago until a mere 11,500 years ago and it could look like a singular occurrence.

However, around fifteen thousand years ago the coldest part of the last ice age was coming to an end, and the climate of the key landmasses north of the equator began to improve. During this time, the Earth's climate repeatedly changed between very cold periods, during which glaciers covered large parts of the world, and very warm periods during which many of the glaciers melted.

I counted 17 cycles between glacial and interglacial periods. The glacial periods lasted longer than the interglacial periods. The last glacial period began about 100,000 years ago and lasted until 25,000 years ago. Right now, we are in a warm interglacial period. These interglacial times played havoc with the development of society and were well outside of any Intervention. Suffice it to say, we are entering the period when history is recorded, whether through writing or passed down stories.

Masamune and Muramasa

A legend tells of a test where Muramasa challenged his master, Masamune, to see who could make a finer sword. They both worked tirelessly, and when both swords were finished, they decided to test the results.

The contest was for each to suspend the blades in a small creek with the cutting edge facing against the current. Muramasa's sword, the Juuchi Yosamu "10,000 Cold Nights") cut everything that passed its way; fish, leaves floating down the river, the very air which blew on it. Highly impressed with his pupil's work, Masamune lowered his sword, the Yawarakai-Te "Tender Hands"), into the current and waited patiently.

Only leaves were cut. However, the fish swam right up to it, and the air hissed as it gently blew by the blade. After a while, Muramasa scoffed at his master for his apparent lack of skill in the making of his sword.

Smiling to himself, Masamune pulled up his sword, dried it, and sheathed it. All the while, Muramasa was heckling him for his sword's inability to cut anything. A monk, who had been watching the whole ordeal, walked over, and bowed low to the two sword masters.

Then the monk explained what he had seen.

'The first of the swords was a fine sword, however it is a bloodthirsty, evil blade, as it does not discriminate who or what it will cut. It may just as well be cutting down butterflies as severing heads. The second was by far the finer of the two, as it does not needlessly cut that which is innocent and undeserving.'

DAY 1 - *Darnell*

As agreed, Abbott helped set up a meeting with Darnell. It was immediate and ahead of the session with Lepton, which was not the order I'd hoped for.

I should have guessed that Darnell would want to meet me somewhere theatrical.

He chose the Colonnade in Rome. I'd not visited this part of Rome for centuries. I remembered it as an extensive collection of imposing buildings rising along the hill. Most were now in ruins. The Rise and Fall of a great Empire.

Under the Roman Empire, the forum had become primarily a centre for religious and secular spectacles and ceremonies, as well as being the site of many of the city's most imposing temples and monuments.

Among the surviving structures I could see the Palazzo Senatoro, various Tempio and distant Basilica, on the way toward the equally ruined Colleseo.

I'd also forgotten just how crazily busy this part of Italy can become, with the mixture of tourists, small Italian cars and natives of Rome mingling together in this sun-baked area.

Abbott had arranged for Darnell to meet me on the steps of the Capitoline Hill, next to the Lupa Capitolina - the She-wolf, which famously had tended Romulus and Remus. I could tell that Darnell's sense of humour had not been displaced by his new powers.

Darnell was with someone else - a splendid woman, carrying a basket, as if she had just returned from the market.

"I wanted you to meet another one like me," said Darnell, "This is Ceres."

I had to wrack my brain for a moment. I couldn't place the name but knew it was powerful.

She smiled at me, and I felt the air around me crackle. I realised she was some kind of super deity.

She spoke to me in informal Italian, "*Ciao - Darnell mi dice che potresti voler unirti a noi qui. Che tu possa anche fare un intervento, anche se penso che i potenti siano già avvenuti.* " - "Hello - Darnell tells me you may wish to join us here. That you may also make an Intervention, although I think the powerful ones have already occurred."

I found I could switch straight into Italian and realised that there were a few extra useful things which I'd picked up along the millennia. I still couldn't remember who she was.

"You don't know, do you?" asked Darnell. I could see he had triumphantly expected me to fail to recognise her.

"Ceres," he continued, "Ceres, the Roman goddess of agriculture, grain, and the love a mother bears for her child. She is the daughter of Saturn and Ops, the sister of Jupiter, and the mother of Proserpine.

I noticed Darnell spoke in the present tense, and simultaneously realised we were in the presence of Ceres.

Now he switched to the past tense, and I realised that some things about Ceres had been lost in the mist.

He continued, "Ceres, the goddess of agriculture, was beloved for her service to humankind in giving them the gift of the harvest, the reward for cultivation of the soil. Also known as the Greek goddess Demeter, Ceres was the goddess of the harvest and credited with teaching humans how to grow, preserve, and prepare grain and corn. She was thought to be responsible for the fertility of the land."

Ceres spoke, and I once more felt the crackle, "It is close to the time of Ambarvalia, when my powers increase, " she explained, "I guess you, as a Watcher for all time, must be used to experiencing some facets of human emotion?"

"No, never," I said. "This is the first time. Ever, it is a most strange sensation if that is what it is."

Now this was making sense. Other gods occasionally dabbled in human affairs when it suited their personal interests, or came to the aid of mortals they favoured, but goddess Ceres was the nurturer of mankind.

Ceres continued, "It is interesting that so few know of my story, yet I brought humanity one of their greatest gifts. The gift of farming and agriculture. I am the sister of Jupiter, and Proserpine was my daughter. Pluto, god of the underworld, kidnapped Proserpine, to be his bride.

"By the time I could follow my daughter, she was gone into the Earth - the underworld.

"To make matters worse, I learned that Pluto had been

given Jupiter's approval to be the husband of his daughter. I was so angry that I went to live in the world of humankind, disguised as an old woman, and stopped all the plants and crops from growing, causing a famine.

"Whoa," I said, "But you were a god before you gifted your intervention to humanity?"

"Not god; it's goddess, we still use the term around here," she replied. "Yes, but nowadays I'm on the same reality plane as Darnell."

My mind was racing as I thought again of the metaverses and the 'branes created by alternative dimensions unseen to humans. Was the underworld another darkened room?

Ceres continued, "Jupiter and the other gods tried to get me to change my mind to stop the famine, but I was determined. Jupiter eventually realised that he had to get Proserpine back from the underworld and sent for her.

"Unfortunately, Pluto secretly gave Proserpine food before she left, and once she had eaten in the underworld she could never leave forever.

"Proserpine is forced to return to the underworld for four months every year. She comes out in spring and spends the time until autumn with me but must go back to the underworld in the winter. The Romans decided it was why plants lose their leaves, seeds lie dormant under the ground, and nothing grows until spring, when Proserpine and I are reunited.

"Cereals," added Darnell, "Think of Cereals - Ceres..."

Darnell was up to his old annoying tricks, and I could see Ceres dig him in the ribs.

"You forget yourself, " she said, and I could feel a different crackle in the air. One I decided was of a mocking directed toward Darnell.

Ceres added, "Darnell and I are different. He acts from self-interest. I try now to act for the good of humanity. Darnell has a string of plans which he will tell you in a moment, of that, I am sure. I performed one deed, driven by family ties, which led to the gift of agriculture."

Darnell added, "But even that has an unintended consequence."

Ceres smiled. "You mean superabundance? I can never see this the way you do, Darnell. Not ever."

With that, Ceres, lifted her eyes towards the sky and then, as we Watchers do, glitched herself away. I felt an overwhelmingly pleasant sensation drain away as I was left with Darnell.

"Don't let her fool you," he added, "Ceres is probably still listening to what we have to say."

"You don't believe in half measures," I said to Darnell, "In the heart of the Roman Empire talking to a Roman super-god."

"Goddess!" said Darnell.

"Goddess, " I quickly corrected.

"The lesson is that one of the biggest interventions ever - agriculture - is hardly even recognised and the instigator of the event - Ceres - is equally lost in the mists. I don't think you need to worry too much, if you cross to this reality."

I'd worked out that Darnell was as crazy as ever. But now there was a new facet. Ceres had mentioned self-interest. I wondered what this could mean.

Darnell looked toward the winding road leading up to the she-wolf statue. Then he waved.

"It's Cardinal; he has also come along at my request."

A gaunt, pale-faced man approached in a long sand-coloured coat which seemed incongruous in the hot Italian weather. I could see that he already knew both Abbott and Darnell.

"Hello," he said - with his gaze directed toward me, "It is best that you don't look directly toward me."

Darnell explained to Cardinal that he was describing Ceres' Intervention, "Ceres had turned things around. Her intervention created a conundrum. People would choose to farm although it did not make for an easy life."

Cardinal interjected, "Ceres intervening to create the rise of agriculture allowed far more humans to be alive. A hunter-gatherer needs about ten square miles of game and berry-filled land to live on, whereas agriculture can produce enough calories in a tenth of that space to keep fifty people alive."

I interrupted, "No wonder Ceres carried a basket overflowing with produce."

Darnell continued, "I'm pleased you noticed the

symbolism. But now for the unintended consequence. The increase in population came after agriculture started, not before. Across the planet vastly more land was inhabited by hunters than by farmers. This is the unrecorded narrative of the Indian forests, the Eurasian steppes, the jungled islands of East Asia and the migrations of the Americas. Most people found ways of not farming. And yet farming was repeatedly invented in completely separate parts of the world.

Cardinal spoke again, "It took nearly ten thousand years from the first attempts at agriculture for the world's population to reach a billion. Now humans are adding extra people at a billion every dozen years. World food stocks, held for emergencies, are tiny. To avoid famine every person needs to be fed by a far smaller patch of land than ever before. It is why I am seeking action."

I wondered what this could mean. Ceres had hinted at self-interest.

Cardinal continued again, "Ceres' interventions happened first in the Fertile Crescent, which curves from today's Jordan and Israel, up to Anatolia in today's Turkey, and then back east into Iraq.

"But then it started in northern China. It occurred in Mexico; and independently in the Andes; then in what is now the eastern United States. Thousands of years separate these breakthroughs, but they are Ceres' handiwork."

Darnell added, "Do you see? Humanity had walked into an accidental trap. An unintended consequence from Ceres' gift. Humanity's decisive step had consequences which could never have been imagined, and from which there was no pulling back."

Cardinal continued, "The trap was that settled farming communities produced bigger populations. Even with Late Stone Age technology, each acre of farmed land could support over ten times as many people as each acre of hunted land. It was not simply about food, either. As we have seen, hunting tribes, always on the move, must carry their children. Once people settled down, the birth rate could rise, and it did.

Abbott added, "Larger families meant more mouths to feed, which meant that farming and herding become ever more important. Herds can never be untethered and returned to the wild. The early farming men and women were shorter in stature and more prone to disease– because parasites and pests settle down as well."

Darnell added, "They cannot stop. Before, they were shaping and taming the plants and animals; now the plants and animals are shaping and taming them, too."

Cardinal continued, "They also had to develop other skills. They had to grind and sift their grain and store it. Their precious domesticated animals, which had to be protected from wild beasts and allowed to wander for food – but not too far – must be exploited in every way. Wool could be sheared and carded and woven. Blood could be drawn off and used to enrich meal. Some farmers developed the habit of drinking the milk of lactating goats and cows – and most of their European descendants remain lactose-tolerant to this day."

Cardinal was on a roll now. "The preparation of hides, the weaving of ropes to help with ploughing, and making baskets and pottery for storing or cooking grain – Think of it - a whole new world of domestic jobs and skills emerged.

"By around eleven thousand years ago, groups of humans realised that by keeping some animals near by–the ancestors of today's sheep, goats and pigs–they could ensure for themselves meat and hides.

Cardinal shifted his gaze toward me, "People had probably been gathering edible seeds for centuries before they planted them, then returned to the same place for the annual harvest of seed-heavy grasses or nutrition-rich peas."

Darnell spoke again. "In societies where men would be expected to hunt further from their settlements, the breakthrough discovery prompted by Ceres was made by women. There are supposedly fifty-six edible grasses growing wild in the world—cereals like wheat, barley, corn and rice."

Cardinal took over, "Additionally, the people of the Fertile Crescent had at their disposal a disproportionate number of the thirteen large animals that can be domesticated."

Then Cardinal's brow furrowed. "They had not only pigs and nearby wild horses but also cows, goats and sheep, plus thirty-two of the edible and grain producing grasses. In the Fertile Crescent, people called Natufians could gather grain around thirteen thousand years ago; and early on—presumably to stay close to the precious grain—they settled down in villages rather than moving around as hunter-gatherers."

Darnell again, "All this gave humankind a surplus of energy no mere predator could hope for. Using it, humans grew from family groups to tribes to villages to cities to nations, allowing them to change much more of the original environment. Humans altered the courses of rivers and dug into the mineral covering of the planet, pulling out coal, oil and gas to provide more power, exploiting ancient vegetable reserves that lived and died long before they arrived."

"And that is where Cardinal's idea came in," said Darnell excitedly.

"Exactly," said Cardinal. "The villages had to come together, to create and then to maintain the complicated system of waterways and dykes needed for agriculture. I showed them a ruling system."

Abbott continued, "Workers had to be organised; the improvements to farming produced surpluses of grain and Cardinal's intervention allowed the introduction of rulers and priests, who developed religions, temples and employed servants to tend them.

He added, "A system of notation and recording developed into a system that could record stories and ideas. Individual families or villages were far too small and had too little spare time to achieve what was needed. Only by combining in large numbers, organised by managers, could they survive. The managers seem to have been priests, or at least to have been based in the temples, from where they oversaw vast irrigation projects."

Abbott added, "Once the system of labour and specialised skills was in place, the managers had access to the brawn to build ever greater temples. The feedback from successful irrigation to the power of those who directed it is obvious: over time, the managers could claim they spoke for, with, and to, the gods."

Cardinal's turn now. I could see they were operating as if a single being, with Cardinal having the main ideas and Bishop running a kind of follow-up explanation.

Cardinal explained, "These priests and rulers handled the settlement's very survival. The original ruling class, high on their platforms, ears tilted to the heavens, had arrived. Below them, totting up the deliveries of grain, beer, meat, and metals they required from the toilers, were the scribes or middle management. You cannot have a hierarchically organised society without the bureaucracy"

Cardinal continued, and I could see where this was leading.

"Priests demand their special places–intimidating, nearer the gods. This required huge numbers of workers and full- time artisans, as well as measuring and planning. That meant detailed notetaking, indeed writing. Then, large tributes of food, beer and raw materials were called for, to keep the building workers alive."

I could see how it was falling into place: Priests of religion. Large-scale building projects. Writing. Taxes. Soldiers. Kings.

The ability to make war.

Darnell, with Cardinal and Abbott, had hastened war's arrival.

But the set of conditions is broader than all-out warfare and all arrived in human history alongside one another, based on the first cities - really the first concentrations of stored wealth, themselves based on riverside farming cultures that needed to work together to tame nature.

This is the shift that is more powerful than the old ties of clan, kin and lineage, and marks the next important moment in human development after Ceres brought farming.

Darnell hastened the rivalry between cities and people, which sped up change, until full-scale war brings catastrophe.

The rise of trained bureaucrats, with their cuneiform writing implements, permitted different people with different languages to communicate; Sumerian becomes the lingua franca for Mesopotamia, and scribes become bilingual. A momentum is under way, which may be lost here or there but which has never stopped since.

The first cities also nurtured a flowering of abstract thought. The ruling class of kings and priests had time to speculate, not least about the mysterious world of winking lights and movements overhead that had also obsessed the builders of Stonehenge.

It is no surprise that Mesopotamia gave us mathematics, both the simple sums to tally trade and taxes and the more complicated ones used to track the stars. Looking up, the Sumerians and Babylonians wondered about this nightly message, with its shapes and regular patterns. If the gods were able to send messages back to them, were these the divine writing? Was there a pattern, which could then be imposed on the rhythm of human life?

Reading the stars required measurement of angles. The Sumerians plotted the movements of the five planets they could see—Mercury, Venus, Mars, Jupiter, and Saturn—and named a day after each. They then named one day after the Moon and another after the Sun, giving them a seven-day week. They regarded seven as a perfect number; and the Sumerian week is of course still the human week, its days still named in the Sumerian fashion.

The Sumerians also developed a counting system based on the number sixty, which is divisible by eleven other numbers and so particularly handy for Bronze Age accountancy. From this derived the 60-second minutes, 60-minute hours, 360-day years and 360-degree circles.

All of this is remarkable enough, but the first cities also brought a flowering of art and design, with alabaster carvings and mosaics and useful stamp-seals for parcels of goods from Uruk, plus inlaid gaming-boards, musical instruments, and delicate gold jewellery from Ur—even before the carved reliefs of the Assyrians and Babylonians.

Today, thanks to the habits of nineteenth-century archaeologists, the loveliest of these things can be found in Berlin and (controversially) London, not in Iraq. Each Mesopotamian city had its own gods, culture, and reputation. Uruk was famous not only for its huge ziggurat and sky-god but for its sexy female deity Inanna, who was associated with all kinds of fertility and whose rites shocked one Babylonian writer: 'Uruk . . . city of prostitutes, courtesans and call-girls - the party-boys and festival people who change masculinity to femininity.'

These first cities are among the most important sites in the human story. Successive floods have reduced many of them to gritty stumps, and obliterated others. Neglect, war, and the lack of interest of later cultures followed by aggressive, treasure-hunting Victorian archaeology has meant that while some of their greatest carvings and other artefacts are in European museums, the sites themselves are often dusty disappointments.

This is tragic, since the achievements of the Sumerians, Akkadians and early Babylonians were huge, and in some ways much more impressive than those of the better-known Egyptians. Their city culture was bureaucratic and clearly in some ways oppressive, weighing heavily on farmers, requiring payment in return for the canals and wells that kept their fields so fertile.

It allowed the emergence of kings with enough muscle to go to war against one another, and to carve out the first empires, along with the misery that early mass-killers such as Sargon of Akkad brought to the land. But these first cities were also places of beauty, intellectual advance, wonder and a great deal of not very innocent fun.

It was Abbott who delivered the ominous summary, "Making people pay tributes as taxes would not have been pleasant; force would have been needed. All the accumulating wealth would be a temptation to robbers and ultimately to rival cities. Therefore, walls were built and some men given the job of full-time protectors. A warrior class emerged. Nothing has advanced technical progress faster than war. "

It left me to wonder how knowingly Darnell, Cardinal and Abbott had provided the worst kind of Intervention. That of warfare.

But this was where it ended. Like a fairground toy that has run out of money, the scene suddenly dimmed. I realised I had consumed my first day. Never had I experienced the feeling of wanting a day to last longer.

DAY 2 - *Lepton & Lekton*

I didn't have long to think about what had just happened. I was suddenly in a dingy apartment reeking of decaying fish. I was in China, in a makeshift wooden room above a market. I'd been sent here by Lepton, who was the second person I'd asked to consult about creating an intervention. Originally, I'd hoped to meet Lepton first, but Limantour was working her chaos as usual.

I looked around. The building was rudimentary, and there were baskets and plastic crates in the corridors. As I looked through the clear plastic lid of one crate, I could see large, rough-skinned red fishes, still alive and gasping through mouths the size of small plates, revealing searing blue tongues.

Then I noticed the next crate. I thought it was rats at first, but then realised it was agitated bats, trapped inside the crates.

Just like when I was in Italy, I could read and understand the Chinese writing. This was Huanan, or Southern China, and all the crates seemed to have shipping labels, outbound from Hankou Railway Yard and then to varied destinations. I wondered about refrigeration and food safety, when, with a flickering of the lights, Lepton and another stranger appeared.

Lepton beamed when he saw me. "Hello, Farallon, it has been a long time! You asked to see me and to witness for yourself that I have continued to enjoy a good living beyond your metaverse."

I looked around and the stranger was also smiling, although his smile looked as if he had been told to look happy in my presence.

"Hello," he said, "My name is Lekton."

I could see what Lepton had done. Lepton was the originator of one of the earliest interventions - the provision of light for the universe. Lekton was almost the opposite. Watchers knew that Lekton's intervention was to bring warfare to humanity. I was standing with the bringers of Light and Darkness.

I decided to deflect matters whilst I considered my options.

"Well, it is an honour to meet you both, although I am not sure of our location?"

"This is the workshop of Scheppach," explained Lekton, "She lives outside of the law around here"

"In what way?" I asked, realising that I could not be in any danger from the human world.

A new voice cut in. Heavily accented, not of China, but of Germany. A slender woman with blue-tinted spectacles appeared from the shadows. She was wearing a form-fitting light-brown well-worked leather apron.

"Farallon, it is my pleasure to meet you," she said, "I am Scheppach, and I import the finest quality knives, which can be used in the wet market below."

I noticed in her short blonde hair; her earrings were formed as two precise tiny daggers. She also had the slender, controlled hands of a concert pianist.

I remembered something about Bladerunners. They were the outlaws who smuggled micron-fine-bladed surgical knives. These knives were used for off-grid operations on humans as well as to augment the combat skills of the warrior classes. The importation was more commonly referred to as smuggling and the kind of person would be correctly thought of as an arms dealer.

I'd been in the room long enough to get acclimatised, and I could see other bulky black cases stacked up beyond the wet fish. I realised from their markings that they were gun safes. I saw Scheppach notice my reaction.

"Yes, you'll see I have a supply of armaments ready for export,"

I knew she meant for trafficking.

Scheppach continued, "This is a useful location to keep others' eyes away. They can't abide the stench from the market and, well, you can see that the way the market operates is barely legal.

"Once we have access to the construction details for the weaponry, we can easily ask the Chinese factory towns to take on the production of as many units as our clients need. The RPG-7 is a case in point. We have supplied 80,000 of these 40mm grenade launchers to Iraq and Afghanistan battlefields. They are badged as 'Made in the USA' and machined out of ordnance-grade steel instead of castings in the way of the original Russian designs from the 1960s. Now we are designing factories to build copies of entire warplanes, based upon stolen

American designs."

I decided there was more darkness than light in this room.

Scheppach added, "Oh yes, and we produce Katana swords too, but with modern steel instead of the pig iron of the Samurai. Masamune would approve if the technology had been available in his time."

I could see outside of the apartment through the grime-caked windows. I wanted to be on the other side of the glass, away from what I could only think of as psychopaths.

Lekton spoke, "You should see now that whatever happens, you get placed in our metaverse after your intervention. I'm sure you have seen that for Darnell, Cardinal, Abbott, Lepton, and myself, it becomes a rewarding journey.

I looked toward Lepton, deciding he was the most beneficent of all of them. I could see a sadness in his eyes. "I've still to visit most of the 84,000 edges of the universe," he said, cryptically.

I realised he was describing the Chinese Courts of Hell - after the Chinese Diyu stories or the Japanese Yomi. It left me with another feeling washing over me like when Ceres had been close, except this time I realised I was experiencing dread.

Lepton continued, "We decided to meet here but our plans call for a journey to Knossos. But first you needed to see the wet market. A precursor symbol of what is happening, used as an excuse. The excuse used to mask the creation of a global pandemic. Humankind resolves it but take no heed of the implied consequences. The huge and unsubtle warning to humanity does not work. We know, we can see forward. We don't need the powers of a scryer. We can run forward on the rails of time."

"Except they stop, " said Scheppach, "Very soon. A few hundred years into the future."

"That's right," said Lekton. "For all of us. We can't see past the event horizon."

"What event?" I asked.

"That's what we need to discover," said Lepton. "I brought light, but from that point in the future all we can see is darkness."

"So why do we need to travel to Knossos?" I asked, "And why is this market a precursor symbol?"

With that, I could feel a ground rush, as if we were in a minor earthquake. The shakes subsided and a bright, hot daylight suddenly bathed us all. I realised we had moved to Crete, and the air filled with the scent of jasmine and oregano, replacing the rankness of the fish market in Huanan. I noticed how all of us, even Scheppach, took it in their stride. I had wondered about Scheppach, because she was not a Watcher, but had become implicated through Lekton.

Scheppach answered, she was smiling, "For all of your time here, you don't seem to have learned much about the ways of the Earth. How it tries to self-heal,"

"And Knossos here. It has been the hub of civilisation," answered Lepton, "The Minoans were the first European civilisation from around 3600 to 1160 BC. Their island of

Crete lies in the far south of the Greek peninsula. They were trading and seafaring people, whose pottery turns up in Egypt and whose art was influenced by the Egyptians."

Lekton added, "Their art and architecture are instantly attractive, giving an initial impression of a tranquil, female-dominated society whose palace walls ripple with dancing dolphins. Amid the fat red columns are images of a little bull-dancing here, a moment of saffron-gathering there. But the Minoans are useful as a warning about history and how we romanticise it."

"But I remember Santorini's earthquake blasting a hole in that part of the Mediterranean?" I said, "Isn't Knossos a reconstruction?"

Lekton continued, "Correct. Knossos only dates to between 1905 and 1930. It is a reconstruction of a Bronze Age palace, filled with fake pictures. It was the lifetime achievement of a rich British archaeologist, Sir Arthur Evans.

"Evans supported the ruined buildings he was excavating with wood and plaster, and then slowly began to 'improve' them with the flexible and useful recent invention of reinforced concrete.

"The extent to which his re-imagining of the Knossos complex is an accurate and reasonable guess, or merely a modernist fantasy, divides even the experts. Evans commissioned modern artists to retouch ancient wall paintings so comprehensively that they produced new ones.

"So, from this rubble, what can we know for sure about the people we call Minoans? Their civilisation lasted for around thirteen hundred years and survived a whole series of natural disasters, including a hugely destructive earthquake and two volcanic eruptions.

They traded tin, very well made and painted pottery, as well as a wide range of foods, oils and other staples. Their agriculture was sophisticated, and it seems that their religion was dominated by priestesses and bull-worship.

"But what warning from the Minoans?" I asked.

Scheppach was shaking her head, "Don't you see? There is a darker side to the Minoan culture. Lekton's intervention pushed them into war and taught them to protect their units with citadels and defensive walls. I could only assist with my infinite supply of increasingly technological weapons. Back then it was spears, Right now we are moving into the era of rail-guns and satellite enforcement systems."

Lekton continued, "Far from being a society of peace and love, wafting about in gossamer and admiring the dolphins, the Minoans became bloody but calculated with it. As the first civilisation in Europe, they combined beauty, human sacrifice and military planning with a class system and fighting elites."

Lekton added, "You could say, with my intervention, they invented war."

Scheppach continued, "And then, through Lekton's interventions, Earth suddenly had a way to correct imbalances of humans. For me, it has been immensely profitable."

"But you are not a Watcher?" I asked, looking towards Scheppach.

"No, correct. I am a mercenary- a soldier of fortune. With Lekton's technologies, I can profit greatly from Earth attempting to rebalance - and Lekton has provided me with longevity, so my operation spans from Cyrus the Great and his Persian Empire conquests at the expense of some 100,000 souls."

She looked wistfully into the air and then towards Lekton. I couldn't believe I was looking at the two people responsible for the slaying of so many. We had been walking through the ruins of Knossos. I was struck by the paintings of bull-leaping and varied figural frescoes, but there were few pictures of conflict. Just like Knossos lacked warfare depictions, Lekton and Scheppach had been suppressing the imagery of warfare. One immense edit.

Then Lekton relaxed a little, "It makes the campaigns of Alexander the Great look small, with around 150,000 deaths, particularly before the Punic Wars killed 1.5 million. Put another way, ten times as many to go to their deaths."

Scheppach added, "And don't let Knossos and the Minoan flower-children fool you. Their peace and freedom came at the price of great conquests. I helped them design long swords and shields. They even devised a signet ring to show they were from the fighting elite, much the way that a current day US Marine wears their ring with pride.

"But how could anything good have ever come from all of this fighting?" I asked.

Lekton looked toward Scheppach again, "If my original intervention was about protection and security, we learned that the unintended consequence was around greed, profiteering and control."

"But it was too late?" I asked.

"The situation accelerated," said Lepton, who had been quiet until this point, "The Three Kingdoms War in China killed around 40 million in the period between the foundation of the state of Wei in 220 and the conquest of the state of Wu by the Jin dynasty in 280, some 60 years later.

Lekton added, "Yes, and there were other big wars in China, like when the Tang Dynasty China and Islamic Empire fought the Yan state in 755, causing a further 13 million deaths in the An–Shi Rebellion."

Scheppach added, "Then there were the Mongol invasions and conquests which took place during the 13th and 14th centuries, killing 40 million and creating the Mongol Empire, which by 1300 covered large parts of Eurasia. Historians regard the Mongol devastation as one of the deadliest episodes in history. It is when humans learned about biological warfare, as the Mongol expeditions spread the bubonic plague across much of Eurasia, helping to spark the Black Death of the 14th century."

Scheppach continued, "And it brings us back to the agrarian economy - back to the farming intervention of Ceres. The Mongol Empire was a land power, fuelled by the grass-foraging Mongol cavalry and cattle. Most Mongol conquests and plundering took place during the warmer seasons, when there was sufficient grazing for their herds."

Lekton added, "Yes, every soldier tended four armoured

horses for interchangeability and speed. No small wonder that the rise of the Mongols was preceded by 15 years of wet and warm weather conditions that allowed favourable conditions for the breeding of horses. This which greatly assisted their expansion - although Scheppach did not profit so much in those days of Genghis Khan's violent cavalry."

Scheppach replied, "I'm not so sure. They had gunpowder and could build bombs. Someone had to show them the way. They also set chains across the harbour, to wreck ships and used firebombs to set fire to all manner of things. Then they got the level of nitrate correct and were able to create the early hand cannons which fired devastating shot across the enemy."

Lekton added, "Just another 300 years later and we saw, in 1519 to 1632, the Spanish cutting their way across the Aztecs in Mexico, then through the Yucatán and the Incas in Peru. Another 12 million casualties from those three related campaigns.

"And then the French religious wars, totalling some 4 million casualties which pales into insignificance contrasted with the further Chinese Wars in 1616–1683 as the Qing China vs. Ming China vs. Shun dynasty, totalled some 25 million deaths."

Lepton said, "It makes the American Revolutionary War seem minor with its 37 thousand deaths."

Scheppach added, "And the Chinese hadn't finished yet. The Taiping Rebellion between 1850-1864 saw another 70 million deaths as Qing China fought the Taiping Heavenly Kingdom. As a context, the American Civil War between 1861–1865 saw around 1 million deaths."

Lekton continued, "We'll jump forward to World War I, which saw 16 million deaths plus a further 24 million through the Spanish flu pandemic, which was exported to Spain from a Kansas war-room barracks. And then approaching 85 million deaths from World War II."

Scheopach added, "But we are seeing a shift now. Earth was able to keep itself balanced through increasingly vicious warfare. Now we are seeing a mixed effect. Part of it is through warfare, but this has been hybridised by the onslaught of other methods, such as the biological one. 230 million cases of COVID and around five million worldwide deaths from the disease."

Lekton spoke, "Earth rebalances, seeking a new equilibrium."

Lekton was stuttering, like a poor-quality video, and I knew I had run out of time. That's a feeling I'd never experienced until this week.

Declare independence!

Declare independence!
Don't let them do that to you!
Declare independence!
Don't let them do that to you!

Start your own currency!
Make your own stamp
Protect your language

Make your own flag
Make your own flag
Raise your flag (higher, higher!)
Raise your flag (higher, higher!)

Declare independence!
Don't let them do that to you!

Damn colonists
Ignore their patronising
Tear off their blindfolds
Open their eyes

With a flag and a trumpet
Go to the top of your highest mountain and
Raise your flag (higher, higher!)
Raise your flag (higher, higher!)

Declare independence!
Don't let them do that to you!
Declare independence!
Don't let them do that to you!
Raise the flag!

Björk Guðmundsdóttir

DAY 3 - *Limantour*

My third day, and I was looking forward to meeting Limantour. I'd saved her until last because I wanted to amass some facts before I saw her to discuss the Intervention.

I could see the lineage. Ceres had pressed agriculture upon the unsuspecting humans. They evolved from hunter/gatherers to farmers and created such a food surplus that they could safely populate newly established towns and cities.

Then an elite had formed; people who wanted greater power, and Lekton had given them the tools and weapons to achieve this. Intriguingly, the first established civilisation - the Minoans - had swept their fighting under a carpet, at least if we are to believe the reconstructions of Evans, the explorer. I believed Scheppach, who had explained to me about long swords and other forms of assault weapon, evolving much later through rocket propelled grenade launchers towards rail guns.

It had also taught me that writing a history of the Earth is a ridiculous thing to do. Everything gets filtered. The victors write the history books and cast themselves as the righteous. It really was the ghosts writing history books.

Limantour arrived on a skateboard, with a new haircut bobbed white and with light blue streaks which matched her powder blue tee-shirt. She had swapped her shorts from two days ago for tight black trousers, with some kind of block logo running up the legs. She was turning heads. We were in Santa Barbara, just along from the pier. I wondered if she had made her way along the Pacific coast, as we were only about 350 miles from where we had first met at Point Reyes.

Limantour smiled, "It becomes about living in wide time and living a long time. I guess you've realised that unassailable information becomes too vast for any individual to absorb? A doom-scroll with the likelihood of immense errors?"

She was right, I'd seen plenty in the last two days but had to piece together my truth.

"C'mon," she said. She flipped her board, grabbed hold of me and whisked me toward Stearns Wharf - the pier structure in Santa Barbara.

"You don't wear any of that body armour?" I asked.

"And the point of that would be what, exactly?"

"As a uniform? So that you don't look - well - unworldly?"

"No, why do you think I wear this hair and these clothes?" she replied, "unless it is to be noticed?"

We were on the boardwalk part of the pier; several cars were driving along it to park. I noticed the slogan on the back of Limantour's tee-shirt, "Off The Wall" and a picture of an anatomical heart.

"Payin' my dues," she said, "Lizzie Armanto - the board rider," she explained. I reminded myself that Limantour was the mistress of chaos theory. She gestured toward a fish restaurant, which looked out onto the calm blue waters of the bay and further towards the Pacific Ocean.

Cormorants with outstretched wings were basking in the sunshine, perched upon the pier's timbers.

Limantour continued talking, although my mind was in a confused meltdown, "We may regard the present state of the universe as the effect of its past and the cause of its future. An intellect which at a certain moment would know all forces that set nature in motion, and all positions of all items of which nature is composed. If this intellect were also vast enough to submit these data to analysis, it would embrace in a single formula the movements of the greatest bodies of the universe and those of the tiniest atom; for such an intellect nothing would be uncertain and the future just like the past would be present before its eyes. Yeah," She grinned at me.

"Don't you see, Farallon? Laplace's demon? Step outside the world to observe the world fully? - Take your brain to another dimension!"

Limantour laughed and said, "Chaos theory may well prevail, where so many minor events can tilt everything, that we are mindful as Watchers of the golden rule never to interfere."

"Is that what you want to prove to me?" I asked.

Limantour answered, "Even in a current event, there are too many sides and perspectives to gain a genuine sense of the truth. Watch politicians swear the sky is any colour they feel like. Or the little self-aggrandised spokespersons sent in to distort and confuse everyone with specious counterarguments."

"I've just listened to a whole series of spokespersons," I said, "Darnell, Cardinal and Abbott, then Lepton,

Lekton...even Scheppach. None of them seemed fully balanced. Even Ceres had a rough time of it, with her daughter partially caught in another dimension."

Limantour continued, "Hold that thought...It should be better that we understand how rulers lose touch with reality, or why revolutions produce dictators more often than they produce happiness, or why some parts of the world are richer than others. It should make it easier to understand how things work."

She added, "But now I must tell you something. About me."

She continued, "I've also, as a Watcher, got a special skill." She was eating a platter of ceviche with sliced jumbo shrimp, jicama, mango, pico de gallo and fresh avocado. I wondered if it was something to do with food.

"I can channel hop. From this human plane of reference to other 'branes. Into other metaverses. And I can, in a limited way, roll backwards and forwards along the timeline."

"Wow. You've never told us, or me, about this?"

"I've told Tomales. She can also jump to other reference planes, but she can't go backwards at all along the timeline. We agreed it was best to keep quiet about it, because otherwise we would be asked to run all kinds of errands."

I could understand this. I'd told very few Watchers about my gravity bending ability. And that was partly because I couldn't think of anything useful to do with it, except party tricks, which were not advisable.

Well, you know about LIGOs, of course?" asked Limantour.

Yes, I knew about LIGOs. LIGO stands for 'Laser Interferometer Gravitational-wave Observatory'. They comprise two enormous laser interferometers located 3000 kilometres apart. LIGO exploits the physical properties of light and of space itself to detect and understand the origins of gravitational waves.

Though the LIGO mission is to detect gravitational waves from some of the most violent and energetic processes in the Universe, the data LIGO collects may have far-reaching effects on many areas of physics including gravitation, relativity, astrophysics, cosmology, particle physics, and nuclear physics.

And, since the "O" in LIGO stands for "observatory", there are unique aspects to its function. LIGO is blind, it is not round and cannot point at a particular part of the sky, and it is rare for a single detector to make a discovery on its own.

The US had built two LIGOs, In Hanford, Washington State and in Livingston, Louisiana. Then a couple of industrial giants had built them, in Bodø, Norway and somewhere in Alaska. And not to be outdone, the Russians had one somewhere to the north of Moscow. Singly, they were of no use. It was only when paired that they could detect anything useful, using triangulation, so it was assumed that either there were secret deals done between LIGOs, or that there were even more in existence.

"But how do you know that any of this intervention will work?" I asked Limantour.

"Have you heard of Holden?" she began, looking at me closely.

"Only as an Australian car brand," I answered.

"Holden is something of a two-edged sword in all of this," replied Limantour.

"Holden has been working to seed a cross-over event between two of the 'branes."

"So has he managed to influence you and Tomales?" I asked Limantour.

"You should meet him," said Limantour. She took both of my hands.

"I'm going to take you across to Holden's metaverse," she said.

I didn't have time to protest, and was suddenly in a white room, decorated with 20th Century Earth furnishings. I knew this was Artificial Intelligence based, and I tried to think of something else to add to the room. A child's rocking horse. Now I could see its head on the other side of the sofa. And maybe some wooden toy train tracks. They were underfoot.

A deep voice spoke, "You are playing with the environment!"

I almost laughed out loud, because Holden seemed to have styled himself on 'Voice of God' television announcers.

Limantour interrupted, "Yes - you have guessed correctly. It is Holden. He wants to take human reality and then - as a sidebar - to bring back knowledge that will allow humanity to self-start its own escape route from the impending disaster."

"How can Holden know about the disaster with such certainty, or about the solution?" I asked. I realised I was speaking as if Holden wasn't there.

Holden answered, "You are correct to speculate that I am a cypher. I operate in another dimension. I can jump from your dimension to other ones and even slide along the timelines."

"With such powers, surely you can get whatever you want?" I asked.

"Precisely," answered Limantour, "Holden has the wish to become a ruler. If the Earth continues upon its current path, then there won't be anything to rule. Holden has seen that, and he knows that the sight lines forward are blocked in a few centuries, as Earth spirals ever further into dystopian decay."

I could see the plot that Holden was creating. Save the world, but then seize control of it.

Holden continued, "I have bypassed the end of the world by riding into an alternative metaverse. I have used my powers to engineer a situation which the human metaverse could comprehend. I have positioned one energy escape route for Earth. It is a series of new knowledge fragments which human minds can use to save Earth."

I was beginning to understand. Holden had created some heavy hints for humans related to scientific knowledge. It would take a discovery of a new source of energy to allow the parts of the original jigsaw fall into place. I was seeing my part in all of this.

"But what if this doesn't work?" I asked.

Holden spoke, "Think about it. Earth is on the road to destruction in any case."

"But how to get the knowledge from your alternate metaverse to the human one?" I asked.

"I have done all of the heavy lifting. By positioning knowledge and even some working examples on the alternate metaverse at roughly the right co-ordinates for a crossover event to cause them to drop into the human metaverse."

"Why can't you just bring them across?" I asked.

"It needs a gravitational distortion to allow the meta verses to cross-over. That's where you come in. You'd bring over the knowledge shards and possibly some other residual 'wash' from the other metaverse. You would do it while you diverted the Hubble Four."

I was thinking of how waves wash up on a beach. The random debris of seaweed and occasional other things that got left behind. It was how I'd imagined the start of the universe, rather than the way the scientists had said.

"Think of it," said Holden, "You'd be restarting everything! Universe 2.0"

"With a few gifts from Pandora included!" I said.

"But most importantly, Earth will have the new knowledge and the means to deploy it," said Holden.

"But only just in time," I added.

"Yes, but Earth is a survivor; you bring the pieces and Earth will know what to do with them."

"And when is this all supposed to happen?"

"We are right on the event horizon," answered Limantour, "you'll need to act almost immediately."

"But I'd need the data if I'm to create a gravity wave, let alone two?"

"I have the co-ordinates for what will be two gravity waves. One for the Hubble redirection and then a second for the crossover event. You'll need to use significant energy for the second event."

I knew there was more to this than Holden and Limantour were telling me.

"So, what else?" I asked, "Like where did you, Holden, get the knowledge?"

"I found another planet, in an alternate metaverse. It exploits magnetomics to create energy and to drive power trains."

"Magnetomics?" I queried.

"Using magnetite to create energy," explained Limantour, "I didn't know about this either."

"But I thought magnetite was found in rocks. That it was iron in origin and fairly magnetic."

Holden answered, "You are right, but that pre-empts one of the devices to make this work. I am altering humankind's understanding of magnetite to mean an additional element which can create extreme energy and can be used to build power-plants, batteries and small motors capable of powering vehicles, with no detriment to the Earth."

I gasped as I realised, "It's because you are bringing something otherworldly into the Earth's metaverse. Something that doesn't belong. It's like tilting the universe."

"Correct," said Limantour, "And that is Holden's genius; except, well, it is you that will be bringing this to the Earth."

"And how will this get to Earth?" I asked.

Holden replied, "I have already prepared packages, 'gifts' if you will, which will land close to major scientific research institutions. The plan is that several places will make simultaneous discoveries and that this will speed up the magnetite discovery program."

I said, "But this could be like da Vinci all over again; where no one will take the lead on any of his discoveries."

"The Cnidarian metaverse I selected is one with interesting properties. I am using its apex predator to spread the knowledge through knowledge shards. Although apex in its current water-bound world, it is still insubstantial on Earth. Think of it like a jellyfish; a member of the Chrysaora. A big mushroom cap, long tentacles along the centre and smaller trailing ones from the cap!" - only larger than any jellyfish known to Earth."

I could feel an inward scream of terror.

Holden continued, "They have a device called nematocysts, which can fire out the knowledge payload - in normal use these are like the barbed stings from the jellyfish. They would propagate the knowledge of magnetomics widely and can also suppress counter-thought."

I kept thinking of the unintended consequences of letting mind-controlling jellyfish with a barbed secret payload loose on Earth.

Boundary Condition

I could hear Holden's fusion rate boosting after the last few moments of interchange. He was hoping to outrun our thought processes, by speeding up his own. Much like a fly sees a human with a swatter as if in slow motion.

Holden spoke, "You are thinking about what happens if we can't control the Chrysaora? We thought of that. It is why we have already introduced DAARQ monitoring. Distributed, Artificial Intelligence, Augmented Reality and Quantum computing. These military systems will monitor for sophisticated intrusion detection and self-protection mechanisms if the Chrysaora - or anything else for that matter - get a foothold. The principle of is that of a Doomsday sensor and it is already used in my other reality. It has been running ever since the US scientists built the first two LIGOs, back in the mid 1990s. The humans have simply not realised how it can be used,"

"In intersecting two meta verses, we knew we must use similar safeguards here on Earth. All we need to do is identify if a boundary condition is crossed."

I was confused, "Boundary condition?"

Holden answered, "Yes the conditions that create triggers for other events."

I asked, "Is that what the LIGO was about? - A condition?"

Holden answered, "The LIGO is watching for a certain condition here on Earth. It can check that the condition of Earth is still viable. If it detects a problem three times in a row, it will invoke the Apex."

"The Apex?" I queried.

Holden answered, "Yes, there's a set of conditions that re-establishes a dominant strain on Earth, on an 'if all else fails' basis. And the apex will function until it has reasserted an equilibrium that ensures the continuation of Earth. Why do you think the dinosaurs became extinct? No true Apex meant that Earth's environment was overly chaotic.

Limantour smiled, "Exactly. it is supposed to be an Earth countermeasure if the planet is attacked, or a new war is creating mutually assured destruction."

"But then there would need to be the second trigger?" asked Sam.

"Correct," said Holden, "That explains the LIGO. It listens for the end of the world, so that it can be triggered as a one-time event. It listens for a pulse - like a heartbeat from Earth. When it's received, all is good, otherwise expect Kratos to exert itself and generate a new Apex.

I thought this was 'a damned if you do and damned if you don't' situation.

My options seemed to be:

A) Let the Earth sputter out;
B) Intervene but set up an Earth self-defence using LIGO which could also terminate everything.
C) The slimmest chance that Limantour's plan might work, even if it was guided by a megalomaniac.

I reviewed the options in my mind. These had not been inspiring days.

Day One, I'd met Ceres who seemed like a breath of fresh air, introducing farming to the world. Darnell, Cardinal and Bishop had exploited this situation to incorporate groups of dwellings which could be controlled and taxed.

Then on Day Two, I'd met the promoter of darkness, Lekton, who had decided to introduce warfare to the world.

Day Three, I'd met the chaotic Limantour, and observed the madness of Holden, who had the created the Intervention Plan, but with many downsides. I'd also discovered that, for some of the Watchers, it was possible to bridge across to another metaverse.

I wondered why I was not getting 'end of meeting' jittering like the first two days.

Limantour sensed this and said, "You won't get end of day phaseouts from me. Remember where we are. Santa Barbara is on the same ley line as the one we started in Point Reyes. Indeed, there are several things about Santa Barbara which are kept special.

She pointed back from the Wharf toward the town.

"The Mission is, of course, on El Camino Real, between

Mission San Buena Ventura and Mission Santa Ynez. And the roads in Santa Barbara are not always a true grid, because they have been realigned to Native American Chumash monuments. Further toward Santa Monica, the Burro Flats pictographs also include predictions of winter and summer solstices and the billenial calendar there incorporates suggestions not of Earth's end, but of Earth's reboot.

Limantour decide to throw me a rationalisation, "Farallon, you have to remember there are no abstract forces in history. Everything that brings change is natural. Climatic shifts, volcanoes, diseases, currents, winds, and the distribution of the plants and animals have shaped humanity.

But most history has been made by human choice and human endeavour. Made by individuals, acting inside their societies. This is where we come in now. To make a choice for the humans. To protect Earth by providing it with the blueprints and access to the material that will release it from the shackles of organic dependency.

I felt the walls had closed in. I would need to flex my powers to engineer this next intervention. It was as if the mad gangster Holden had made me an offer I could not refuse, via the smooth talk of Limantour.

Limantour looked me directly in the eyes. I could sense that her power must include some kind of soul search.

"You are ready?" she asked, "To do this thing? Tomorrow?"

I nodded.

"No," she said, "You have to answer me directly, with

words...Will you assist the Intervention? Tomorrow? From Paris?"

"Yes, I'll help you tomorrow," I said, "and from Paris, but you will need to tell me where."

PART THREE

Got to keep on moving

Got to keep on moving
To understand both sides of the sky
You got to keep on grooving, yeah
Good grooving
Because you got your God and so do I

Jimi

Paris

Limantour and the others - Drake, Tomales and the still unexpected Abbott met me in Paris the next day. We were in Jardin Des Tuileries. There's a 136-pace wide ley line there which links to the Louvre. It is one of the strongest ley lines, and is on a tourist-travelled white gravelled path. A popular author once wrote about ley lines in Paris, but missed this one, focusing instead on the double pyramid inside the Louvre.

But Limantour knows about ley lines and their adaptations, including the use of crystals to bend their directions. Underneath the Arc de Triomphe de Carrousel, which is the more famous Arch's smaller sibling, there are many buried crystals which divert and split the ley lines.

"Are we here for the ley lines?" I asked.

There was a crackle and a 'voice of God' spoke out again. Holden was back.

"Yes, in a manner of speaking," he boomed, "The configuration here gives us the greatest chance that your gravity waves will be transmitted in the correct directions."

"Correct dimensions!" added Limantour.

I was clutching the single sheet of paper onto which the two sets of co-ordinates had been written by Limantour. Unlike a normal map reference, these were three dimensional. I didn't let on that these were easy for me to manipulate, nor that they lacked the precision that I was used to. Instead, I asked, "Are you certain that this is all I will need?"

To my surprise, Abbott answered, "Yes, we have cross-checked them numerous times. They lack the fine-grained precision you are used to because we didn't know exactly when you would be here. It means you'll make a slightly bigger splash with gravity than is actually needed to accomplish the task."

I sat down on the grass, cross legged.

I would do this thing.

Chaos absorption

I was aware of Limantour as I closed my eyes to set the co-ordinates. She was holding my hands.

"It is my intervention," she whispered, "I want to ensure that you are safe, and that we don't revert."

I could feel her pulse and her breathing. I was getting a similar sensation to when I'd met Ceres; a warmth and comfort which I didn't ever experience except in these last few days.

"I'm guarding you from Chaos," she explained, "If that occurs, we lose everything. Any Chaos will be absorbed into me."

Suddenly it made sense. I was diverting the Hubble Four and about to ripple gravity for the second time. If our plan was to work, we could not let original Chaos re-enter the scene. We need to know that the Earth's dwellers could continue as before and that the plan handed from Holden would unfold in its most linear sense.

I remembered that in the classical Greek world, Chaos was the origin of everything and the very first phenomena that ever existed. Limantour was my guardian across a primordial void - shielding me from the empty unfathomable space at the beginning of time, from which everything was created.

In performing our reset of the Universe, we did not want to send ourselves back to a start condition.

Limantour was whispering to me: "Just think of the Greek gods: Gaia as Mother Earth, Tartarus representing the underworld, Eros for love, Erebus for the darkness and Nyx as night."

She continued, "In the beginning, Chaos was a state of random disorder existing in primordial emptiness, and later a Cosmic Egg formed in its stomach, hatching and producing the first gods into the darkness.

"My Chaos was a space that separated and divided the Earth, where mortal humans lived; from the sky, where the gods lived.

"Remember that Zeus was the Olympian god of the sky and the thunder and was the king of all other gods and humans. He was the son of Cronus and Rhea and was unfaithful to his sister and wife, Hera.

"Zeus spawned many children including Athena for wisdom, Apollo for divinity, Artemis as the hunter, Hermes as messenger, Dionysus for wine, Heracles for bravery, Helen of Troy to protect sailors, Hephaestus for fire, Hebe for youth and Ares for war."

I realised Limantour had seated next to me and talked to me through the entire time when I was sending out the gravity waves. I wondered if anything was different.

I looked to Limantour, she was breathing heavily and I realised it looked as if she had been in combat, all the while protecting me from Chaos. She handed me something. It was five dice.

"Throw them," she asked, "Quickly."

I did, and they landed as five times sixes.

"Again," she asked.

This time all twos.

"Again!"

Five times four.

"Keep throwing them," she asked. She was now gripping my other hand tightly.

This time I threw them and one kept spinning longer than the others. A four and four fives.

Again. One dice bounced away. I had to retrieve it.

Then I threw them all again. Two, two fours, a five and a six.

Limantour's breathing slowed. She smiled and stood.

"Good," she said, "I have absorbed the interdimensional chaos and we have a normal condition here on Earth again."

Limantour had protected me from importing new chaos from the metaverse with which we had intersected. I wished she had told me about this aspect.

"What? to deter you even more?" she asked, reading my thoughts. Limantour was fully recovered.

I looked across toward Abbott.

"Has anything changed?" I asked.

He remained silent.

"Abbott?" asked Limantour. Tomales and Drake looked across to Abbott's position.

Suddenly, Abbott stood.

"I must go," he said, "To check with Holden."

The air around him glitched and he disappeared.

"I guess that means we'll need to find out for ourselves," said Tomales, "Hey, great work, you two!"

Tilted

Je commence les livres par la fin
Et j'ai le menton haut pour un rien
Mon œil qui pleure c'est à cause du vent
Mes absences c'est du sentiment

Je ne tiens pas debout
Le ciel coule sur mes mains
Je ne tiens pas debout
Le ciel coule sur
Ça ne tient pas debout
Le ciel coule sur mes mains

Ça ne tient pas debout
Sous mes pieds le ciel revient
Ils sourient rouge et me parlent gris
Je fais semblant d'avoir tout compris
Et il y a un type qui pleure dehors

Sur mon visage de la poudre d'or
Je ne tiens pas debout
Le ciel coule sur mes mains
Je ne tiens pas debout
Le ciel coule sur mes mains

Ça ne tient pas debout
Sous mes pieds le ciel revient
Nous et la man on est de sortie
Pire qu'une simple moitié

On compte à demi-demi
Pile sur un des bas-côtés
Comme des origamis
Le bras tendu pareil cassé

Tout n'est qu'épis et éclis
Ces enfants bizarres
Crachés dehors comme par hasard
Cachant l'effort dans le griffoir

Une creepy song en étendard
Qui fait

J'fais tout mon make-up
Au mercurochrome
Contre les pop-ups
Qui m'assurent le trône"

Je ne tiens pas debout
Le ciel coule sur mes mains

Je ne tiens pas debout
Le ciel coule sur

Ça ne tient pas debout

Le ciel coule sur mes mains
Je ne tiens pas debout
Sous mes pieds le ciel revient

Ed Adams

I'll die way before Methuselah
So, I'll fight sleep with ammonia
And every morning, with eyes all red
I'll miss them for all the tears they shed

I'm actually good
Can't help it if we're tilted
I'm actually good
Can't help it if we're tilted

I miss prosthesis and mended souls
Trample over beauty while singing their thoughts
I match them with my euphoria
When they said, "Je suis plus folle que toi"

I'm actually good
Can't help it if we're tilted
I'm actually good
Can't help it if we're tilted

Nous et la man on est de sortie
Pire qu'une simple moitié on compte à demi-demi
Pile sur un des bas côtés comme des origamis
Le bras tendu paraît cassé, tout n'est qu'épis et éclis

Ces enfants bizarres
Crachés dehors comme par hasard
Cachant l'effort dans le griffoir
Et une creepy song en étendard, qui fait

I'm doing my face
With magic marker
I'm in my right place
Don't be a downer

I'm actually good
Can't help it if we're tilted
I'm actually good
Can't help it if we're tilted

- Héloïse Letissier

Safe Mode

Now although I haven't really mentioned it much, we Watchers are able to keep up with technology. We can tap into human communications, although we don't have too much need of other services like transportation.

We decided we'd better keep a check on NASA comms traffic to see if they had noticed the Hubble deflection or arrival of knowledge shards. Normally Drake would do this, but I noticed Tomales was on the case.

Tomales spoke, "So far I'm not convinced that they have even noticed the telescope deflection, let alone the imminent arrival of the knowledge shards. Look, would you believe it, the Hubble telescope has entered so-called safe mode. She flipped a report across to each of us.

Hubble Instruments Remain in Safe Mode, NASA Team Investigating

NASA is continuing to investigate why the instruments in the Hubble Space Telescope recently went into safe mode configuration, suspending science operations. The instruments are healthy and will remain in safe mode while the mission team continues its investigation.

Hubble's science instruments issued error codes at 1:46 a.m. EDT Oct. 23, indicating the loss of a specific synchronization message. This message provides timing information the instruments use to correctly respond to data requests and commands. The mission team reset the instruments, resuming science operations the following morning.

At 2:38 a.m. EDT, Oct. 25, the science instruments again issued error codes indicating multiple losses of synchronization messages. As a result, the science instruments autonomously entered safe mode states as programmed.

Mission team members are evaluating spacecraft data and system diagrams to better understand the synchronization issue and how to address it. They also are developing and testing procedures to collect additional data from the spacecraft. These activities are expected to take at least one week.

The rest of the spacecraft is operating as expected.

"Unbelievable," said Limantour, "The one time we need it, the telescope is being repaired."

"That timing is before I generated the gravity wave," I said.
"But look," said Tomales, "It says the rest of the telescope is still operational. Would that be enough?"

I felt the air crackle as Abbott suddenly returned.

"It's deliberate," he said, "The outage was all part of Holden's plan. The change in trajectory of the Hubble won't be detected, although it will still be able to transmit it's diagnostics and findings. It is so that what Farallon has done will not be accidentally course-corrected by the human operators."

"But what about the knowledge shards?" I asked, "I sent the gravity wave exactly as directed."

Abbott smiled, "The second gravity wave is almost irrelevant," he replied, "The reason it was necessary was to provide some apparent causality for the sudden appearance of meteor showers around the Earth. Watch tonight, there will be quite a show. The humans will retro-fit the explanation to the gravity wave."

I realised Holden was playing a deep strategy and had revealed only a part of it to us. I wondered why Abbott seemed to have gained his trust.

I started to wonder if I was becoming trapped in Holden's system. Whether he inhabited a dark room and a science incomprehensible to Earth -bound beings.

They say that there is nothing new under the sun.

Ecclesiastes, the originator of the statement complains frequently in his writings about the monotony of life. The entire passage (1:9) reads,

> *'The thing that hath been, it is that which shall be;*
> *and that which is done is that which shall be done:*
> *and there is no new thing under the sun.'*

Ever Shakespeare in his Sonnet 95 was of a similar mind:

> *'If there be nothing new, but that which*
> *Hath been before, how are our brains beguil'd,*
> *Which labouring for invention bear amiss*
> *The second burthen of a former child.*
> *Oh that record could with a backward look,*
> *Even of five hundred courses of the sun,*
> *Show me your image in some antique book.'*

Of course, Holden's twist was that his sun was a different one from ours. He had now successfully created a linkage from his world to ours. A Trojan horse.

Homer's 5th Century BC tales of the Iliad and Odyssey with their myths of Helen's abduction and the Trojan Horse dug their way into the world's imagination, with influence extending from Roman generals to the poets of Shakespeare's England and modern filmmakers.

But it was the Virgil's Aeneid which described how, after a fruitless 10-year siege, the Greeks at the behest of Odysseus constructed a huge wooden horse and hid a select force of men inside, including Odysseus himself. As a war trophy, it was pulled into Troy, from whence the warriors released themselves to sack Troy.

I was anxious that we had not somehow created history repeating itself, as our unintended consequence, with Abbott lurking with black wings, able to bridge between Holden's powers and the missteps of humanity.

Not only are Homer's stories of a saturation bloodshed war, but they are of an unusually convincing one, about an army whose leaders are petty and sometimes mutinous, where disease stalks the camp and wounds are frightful and the enemy is to be admired, not merely hated.

And in which the good guys die. The Iliad glories in violence yet was written by someone who found the human lust for war stupid and bitter. Homer was deeply conflicted about warfare, a deathless poet of the human condition.

These are the centuries when humankind's core civilizations moved (with Scheppach's commercial zeal) from bronze weapons to CMC-steel ones, and from oral tales to written stories. The role of war as a dark driver of change has been unavoidable. Advances in metalworking, wheels, horsemanship, sailing, mathematics and counting, architecture and religion, have been driven by confrontation – in China, India and the Mediterranean.

I always considered the Iliad an ambiguous story. Greece is a good place to start it, both because of what will happen there and what had happened just before the Iron Age, when we get a tantalising glimpse of a better future that would be snuffed out.

That is what Holden has now promised. A better future for Earth, if only we follow his instructions. But he has kept back some of the key parts. He wants control of the

Intervention, just as he wants control of a surviving Earth.

But I knew the rest of the Iliad's story. Across the Mycenaean Greek world of Homer's heroes, a dark shadow would soon fall, scattering the people, destroying the palaces and cities, until even the ability to write was lost. The Greeks who followed, using Homer to recall their identity, blamed war for their predicament.

Humans do not know quite what happened. Watchers know that around 1000 BC a string of disasters hit the eastern Mediterranean, causing a dramatic depopulation. But that was not all. Invasions of Dorian tribes from the north came upon Greek statelets weakened by local conflicts and wiped them out.

The natural disasters—just like climate change and a series of terrible earthquakes which provoked local wars of mere survival. Who owns the village, the food, the water supply? The answer? Whoever wins the fight for it.

All of this was troubling me now. My first act had been to create the gravity waves. From my new vantage point after that effect, I could see a whole chain reaction could take place, meticulously planned by the power-hungry Holden.

Before the Mediterranean's disaster, the Bronze Age world was booming. Shipwrecks yielded much of the evidence for modern-day historians, illustrating the wealth, sophistication and a cosmopolitan culture that disappeared.

Holden would need to guard against this happening again. He needs to preserve whatever has developed over millennia and not to plunge the Earth into a total restart - prevent an Initial Program Load, if you will.

Limantour interrupted my thoughts.

"Welcome to my world of Chaos," she said.

Just hangin' around

"Don't leave me hangin'," became a stock phrase in the early 21st century. It referred to how people greeted one another with a five-finger elevated splayed handheld forward. The other person was supposed to do the same, resulting in a 'high-five.'

If the recipient didn't return the 'five', then the originator was left hanging. It was how I felt now I'd executed the gravity wave for Holden. I was left hangin'.

Drake had been monitoring comms again.

"Yes, it is being reported as the onetime event known as the meteor shower Comet 24P/Djamma This new meteor shower gets its name from the Iceland-discovered Comet Djamma and there might be a hidden pocket of dust from Comet Djamma that will collide against Earth years from now, but astronomers are still unsure about how, if at all, it could appear then."

"Good," said Limantour, "They have spotted the k-shards."

Drake continued, "They say that a single-shot meteor shower is possible because a dust stream's orbit changes shape and size. Because material enters space after cascading off a comet, the debris cloud's original path through the solar system is the same as the comet's orbit."

"I guess it is useful because once someone has broadcast

about it, then most observatories will want to track the event," said Tomales.

At least part of the plan was working.

Are we going to Bodø? Asked Limantour. "You'll see the Northern Lights and the new meteor shower!"

We checked a location and then flickered across to Bodø, Norway, located just north of the Arctic Circle. Because of atmospheric refraction, there is no true polar night in Bodø, but because of the mountains south of Bodø, the sun is not visible in parts of the municipality from early December to early January.

Drake explained, "It features among the strongest tidal currents in the world, with water speeds reaching 22 knots, is Saltstraumen, about 30 kilometres southeast of Bodø.

Drake continued, "Bodø has a long history with the Norwegian Armed Forces, and especially the Royal Norwegian Air Force (RNoAF). The Norwegian Armed Forces Joint Operational Headquarters are at Reitan, east of Bodø. Parts of NATO air forces attending the annual Cold Response exercise are stationed at Bodø Main Air Station (MAS)."

"So, it is a major military base?" I asked.

Drake continued, "In a manner of speaking. Bodø is also home to the Research and Development arm of Raven Holdings, a major international conglomerate whose subsidiary Brant Industry has created a base for the development of Artificial Intelligence. This includes supplying Bodø MAS with trial equipment."

"Scheppach would be pleased," I exclaimed, "The further computerization of warfare?"

"And conventional force too," continued Drake, "Bodø MAS is a major Norwegian military air base, housing two-thirds of Norway's F-16 fighter force and two of RNoAF's SAR Sea Kings. Bodø, competing with Ørland and Evenes, is a candidate for the Northern Air Base in the new RNoAF system."

He added, "Bodin Leir located near the air station was an RNoAF recruit school, including Norwegian Advanced Surface to Air Missile System personnel and a national response unit. The base was central during the Cold War because of its strategic location and proximity to the Soviet Union.

"It would have been vital in the build-up of NATO air and land forces to defend Norway, and thus the entire northern flank of NATO, in a war with the Warsaw Pact. It could also have been used as a forward base for American bombers to strike targets in the Soviet Union.

"Now Bodin Leir is a camp to house military personnel for The Norwegian Joint Headquarters and Bodø Main Air Station."

"Okay, " I said, "So does this mean we are sending knowledge shards to a war factory?"

"A major military base, run by NATO and next to a huge Raven Holdings Research and Development facility," answered Limantour.

"What could possibly go wrong?" I asked.

Bodø Travbane

The location that Limantour had given to us all was an oval racetrack track about 10 kilometres outside of Bodo. It was called Bodø Travbane and the small building there showed pictures of horses pulling carts around the racetrack.

I could see that Limantour had selected the spot because it was away from people and gave a sensational view of the sky, only interrupted by distant mountains.

Drake had disappeared and now returned with a selection of food items in carrier bags marked with Coop Prix Storgata.

"I thought we'd blend in better if it looked as if we were here for a picnic," he said.

Tomales was already looking through the bags, settling for a banana and bottle of fruit juice. We checked the time. An hour until darkness.

"I got this, " said Drake, pulling a small pair of binoculars from another of the bags.

"Four altogether," he elaborated, "That way, if the shards are small, we'll stand a better chance to see them."

Drake busied himself with checking the communication

system again.

"They are saying the comet tail is one of the largest they have seen. It almost passes as a meteorite collision."

Then we saw it. Suddenly. A huge green light coming down from the sky. We already had the green from the Northern Lights, and now we had this meteorite with Holden's payload about to hit the earth.

To indicate size, it now looked like a second moon, only moving much faster. It was still silent. Then we say a violent flash and the moon shaped object broke into smaller pieces, all speeding toward earth.

Then we heard the rumble, which just kept getting louder. We were experiencing the delay to the sound caused by the distances.

"Wow! Said Tomales, "some display!"

"Not just here," said Limantour, "But also in several other important locations."

Drake nodded. "Yes, the comms is picking out the NASA chatter. As predicted, the k shards are targeting other research and development facilities. Now we just need Hubble to spot the magnetite bearing asteroid and it will be 'Game On'."

"It'll be a waiting game," observed Limantour.

The others nodded.

Cargoes

Quinquireme of Nineveh from distant Ophir,
Rowing home to haven in sunny Palestine,
With a cargo of ivory,
And apes and peacocks,
Sandalwood, cedarwood, and sweet white wine.

Stately Spanish galleon coming from the Isthmus,
Dipping through the Tropics by the palm-green shores,
With a cargo of diamonds,
Emeralds, amethysts,
Topazes, and cinnamon, and gold moidores.

Dirty British coaster with a salt-caked smokestack,
Butting through the Channel in the mad March days,
With a cargo of Tyne coal,
Road-rails, pig-lead,
Firewood, ironware, and cheap tin trays.

John Masefield

She has that razor sadness that only gets worse

So far, I've only remarked obliquely about the gods. Humankind seemed to sense them all by itself, but with a remarkable consistency. Watchers knew we were not gods or super-deities. Our common special power was the avoidance of boredom over exceptionally long periods of time.

Limantour looked wistfully on: "I think we can wait here for a while. The observation systems cannot ignore this much cosmic activity. " She looked deep in thought and flipped the wheels of the roller-skates she'd arrived here on. Drake and Tomales continued to run monitoring of the science station.

I looked at Limantour, "Hey, I thought skates had four wheels?" Take our mind off the wait.

"Not these. Three large in-line wheels. Ideal for the boardwalks and rougher surfaces but still fast on tarmac," explained Limantour.

I decided I couldn't keep up with Limantour's daily change of sport activity.

"But why are you looking like that?"

"Like what? I was just thinking..."

"Abcut...All of this?"

"Yes. I just hope Holden and Abbott haven't played us."

Drake and Tomales looked around, Drake spoke, "Yes, I don't want to be played like an ice puck."

Limantour lowered her voice, "I've sometimes wondered if we were gods, but that we didn't know it."

I smiled. I knew this conversation and where it led from talking to others.

"If we were, would we let it get to this?" I asked, "Earth's endgame being rescued by knowledge from another dimension!"

"I know, it does all seem pretty crazy," answered Limantour, "But you know that is how I survive. Chaos is everything for me."

I answered, "Yes, it is strange that out of this chaos comes so many belief systems that seem fundamentally the same."

She nodded, "I wonder that too, sometimes. After the Hebrews tipped human beliefs to monotheism. A single universal god who has a personal relationship with everyone who believes in him."

I smiled as I remembered a human movie with a comedy star who had become the recipient of global prayer emails to a single being.

Limantour added, "The gods of polytheism, in all their buzzing, boisterous confusion, were within the universe. They were subject to nature. They did not create it. The

Jewish god gave life meaning from outside, and allowed a new politic of the Covenant of a people pledging themselves to one another and to the common good. This new way of understanding would bind people together with a new intensity. "

Tomales called over, "Sadly, it would divide them with a fresh ferocity, too."

We'd all seen this, of course. The Jews spending around four hundred years in captivity in Egypt before breaking free under a leader with an Egyptian name - Moses - and trekking to the Promised Land where they ousted local tribes and settled down. But there are no Egyptian history books to show this, nor any archaeological evidence, and the Old Testament story was written down only some seven centuries later.

We had seen that the Hebrew god was not alone in his universe. El (as in Isra-el) was the father god - like the Zeus - of a divine family. His wife was Asherah, his children were the storm-god Baal, who also brought fertility, and his sister Anat. These all had a significant overlap with the Nordic god-king Zeus, his wife Erah (think ash-Erah) and thunder god Thor.

Of course, there were plenty of stories to accompany these characters, as we see their legends handed down through word of mouth before the written word became commonplace.

The idea of 'god' as a Greek-style being walking on the Earth, speaking and intervening personally in human life faded in favour of a more transcendent, obscure and alarming presence.

This took centuries and is traced by scholars of the oldest

parts of Jewish writing in what Christians now call the Old Testament.

The Assyrian empire, with its huge capital at Nineveh, produced a series of hugely successful warrior kings, who carved out most of the Middle East as their fiefdom through a mixture of intimidation and raw terror-tactics.

Their army was by far the most professional and well-equipped of the age and their punishments for anyone who stood against them included decapitation, flaying alive, impaling and deportation all as depicted on clay tablets and memorialised with stone-slab carvings. War propaganda intended to intimidate visitors to Nineveh.

The Assyrians were eventually to meet the formidable Babylonians, led by their king Nebuchadnezzar. There were two phases to their attack. In the first, the Jewish king and ten thousand of his people were taken into captivity. But this did not finish Judah off. There was a revolt, led in part by the prophet Jeremiah.

The Babylonian army came back in 586 BC for a fearful siege of Jerusalem. After many months of being driven to starvation, the inhabitants were overrun, and the city almost destroyed.

A further twenty thousand people were taken off, not to Nineveh this time, but to Babylon. The Temple where Yahweh had resided was almost obliterated. The famous 'Babylonian exile' during which, by the waters, the captives lay down and wept, remembering Zion, had begun.

For the people of Jerusalem, led east to Babylon, it must have been an exceptional spectacle. It was one of the world's great centres, a melting-pot of Middle Eastern peoples, mingling under its enormous gates, by its dramatic stepped ziggurats, in its temples and hanging gardens. It was a glittering spectacle of blue- and yellow-glazed tiles, statues of bulls, lions and dragons, and great processional roads. Here, sensible exiles would adapt and conform.

The Jews refused. Their scribes and priests consulted written scrolls and decided that Yahweh had not been destroyed with his Temple. Instead, he followed his people like a giant shadow and was with them in their exile. He was with them, however, for only so long as they observed purity laws, which had originally been just for the priests. They must keep themselves apart from heathens.

Slowly, it strengthened into a branding exercise, with different religions putting their stamp on things. The Christians with their cross, itself a symbol of a torture instrument, and other power bases such as the Catholics trying to gain ascendancy.

"Or," said Limantour, "There's Buddhism from India in the sixth century BCE. I wonder sometimes if our state as Watchers is that a kind of Nirvana?"

She paused, saw I was looking confused, and then continued. She could do razor sadness well: "They say that space, time and nature were created naturally, have cycles, survives for a set time, then is destroyed and remade.

"Buddhists believe everything depends on everything else, and everything is interconnected. Present events are caused by past events and become the cause of future events. Buddhism is human-centred and states that existence is endless because individuals are reincarnated repeatedly, experiencing suffering throughout many lives."

Limantour was on a roll, "Only achieving liberation, or 'nirvana', can free a human being from the cycle of life, death and rebirth. Buddhism has six realms into which a soul can be reborn. From the most to least pleasant, these are:

"Heaven, the home of the gods (devas); which is a realm of enjoyment inhabited by blissful, long-lived beings. In this realm of nirvana, life is a continual round of pleasure and enjoyment, with no suffering, anxiety or unfulfilled desires; and where human beings are rewarded for many past good deeds."

She smiled and then continued, "Then there is the realm of humanity. Although humans suffer, this is considered the most fortunate state, because humans have the greatest chance of enlightenment. In this realm, passionate and perceptive human beings experience many states of mind and have the most opportunity to free themselves from the cycle of death and rebirth, and hence progress to the heavenly realm."

Limantour flicked the wheel on one of her skates, "Now we reach the realm of the Titans or angry gods (asuras); these are warlike human beings who are at the mercy of angry emotional impulses."

She looked around, "Then the realm of the Hungry Ghosts (pretas); these unhappy human beings are bound to the fringes of human existence, unable to leave because of particularly strong attachments. They are unable to satisfy their craving, symbolised by their depiction with huge bellies and tiny mouths."

She grimaced, "Then it is the Animal realm. Undesirable because animals are exploited by human beings and do not have the self-awareness to achieve liberation. This is a life of ignorant complacency and dullness, in which one does not look beyond avoiding pain and seeking comfort."

Now she looked as if it was the end of what she was describing: "The Hell realms. People here are horribly tortured in many creative ways, but not forever, only until their bad karma is worked off. This is a claustrophobic place of extreme hot or cold in which human beings cannot escape the torment of their own intense anger and hate."

"It's a conundrum," I said," deciding where Watchers are among these realms."

"No," answered Limantour, looking tormented, "Remember, we are outside of all of this. Outside of human imposed belief systems. It is through this that we can investigate what is happening to the Earth and the Universe. We Watchers come out of nothingness to enjoy a spectacle which remains quite indifferent to us."

I knew what Limantour meant, living outside of Earth's systems, but I was also aware of the actions being developed by Holden and coat-tailed by Abbott. To exploit the end of everything, via a manipulated reset.

Deviate

We'd been at the Travbane for a couple of hours by now. We didn't want it to go over five hours with us all together, because we'd exceed the maximus and be randomly re-distributed around the World.

Suddenly Tomales called out, "It's happened! They have seen the effect of the Hubble deviation. They are piecing it together but believe that the Hubble has found magnetite in that asteroid, and that it originates from Jupiter's moons."

"Now they need to realise it can only be from Ganymede," said Drake, "This is where the knowledge shards come into play."

Then, Abbott reappeared, like spectre. He was still all in black and could easily have been mistaken for a ghoul.

"It's okay, " he said, "The Chrysaora landing has worked. They have fired their nematocysts, containing the knowledge payload. There are plenty of scientist walking around now who already know how magnetomics works."

I looked at Limantour. It was as if humankind had just received an injection from another dimension. I worried it was from a dark room which humankind has steadfastly avoided.

Abbott continued, "Of course there are some details to this knowledge finding. First, it will take Earth maybe 20 years to develop the technology beyond its first iteration. However, some of the regular space missions from Earth can be repurposed. Instead of launching new satellites for better surveillance, they can be re-engineered and provide the first missions to Jupiter. It will take around eleven earth years to reach Ganymede, and the only option is for countries of Earth to work together to make this possible."

Tomales asked, "Is this Holden's plan? And did you know about it all along?"

Abbott answered, "I know it now, but I don't think I knew it before I reached Bodo. There is a net being drawn around parts of earth and it inhibits certain memories, and certain types of thought."

Limantour and Tomales looked concerned by this revelation. Tomales asked, "So an unintended consequence of the Chrysaora-based knowledge shards is some kind of neural shield?"

Abbott grimaced, "I wish I could say it was unintended, but I think Holden knew all along. He had told me he needed to focus minds on creating the space-trains to bring back magnetite. That it would require some level of control of minds to achieve this."

I could also feel a numbness affecting my memory. I wondered whether it was a side-effect from the neural shield. Alongside I could feel new ideas developing. Small motors capable of driving large craft. Batteries that required almost no recharge and yet whose charges did not deplete their capacity by more than tiny amounts. Then it flipped to other topics. Blood management in humans. Nano-engineering on the human body and a myriad of smaller ideas.

"Is this affecting you?" asked Limantour.

I nodded, "Yes, I'm being affected. Maybe I'm being infected. The nematocysts from the Chrysaora are doing something. I'm learning about new things, but I fear I am also forgetting some others. It is like there is someone probing around in the back of my consciousness."

Tomales nodded, "Me also, and I'm wondering if it can effect Watchers this much then what effect will it have on humans?"

Drake answered, "I've still been monitoring the normal airwaves. They have gone crazy."

He continued, "Raven Holdings have already announced that they will support a new blood management system to protect humankind from various predicted illnesses. They say they have been working on something for years, which is now ready to be launched. Cartridge based tropus which will both manage blood heath and which can be used to introduce nanoparticles into a body to provide healthcare services."

"And that is not all. They are calling it a Great Leap as several companies have announced new space craft which would be capable of reaching Jupiter."

"Finally, there have been some great strides in Artificial Intelligence, allowing vastly improved cybernetics to be included on the spacecraft."

I wanted to suspend disbelief that these items were occurring together, but I could feel that my critical faculties had been numbed. I could only accept what I was being told at this firehose speed.

Limantour spoke to me quietly, "We have been infected in the same way as Earth. I'm guessing that we will be further manipulated as this goes forward."

I nodded. I noticed Abbott didn't seem to be at all concerned by any of this. Then I realised Holden must have taken control of Abbott earlier.

Limantour took my hand in her right hand and Tomales with her left hand. She whispered to Drake," Stay here dear Drake, we will be back before you know it."

Drake nodded his assent.

I felt the vibration of us moving to another location, still in the northern hemisphere. We were in the United States again, but this time I could see the car tags mainly said The First State - Delaware.

We were looking out to a placid river and Limantour told me we were in Wilmington.

Limantour spoke, "It's where much of the gunpowder and then ships and other war-related goods were created. You could say that the city prospered from the surrounding wars."

"But why bring us to Delaware?" I asked. Tomales was also looking enquiringly toward Limantour.

"I've looked at the next few decades," answered Limantour, "An area - the so named New Delaware - becomes a hub for much of what happens."

"I thought the visibility was blocked. Like it marked the end of the world?" I asked.

"It was, but ever since those gravity waves, things are clearing. I think you brought about a bridging between the universe's metaverse and another one brought to us by Holden."

"I think I've been able to cross some artefacts from that other place into our universe," I corrected.

I was thinking of how a gravity wave was like a wave of water washing the shore and bringing debris with it. Except this debris was from another dimension. It only crystallised that my theory of the beginning of the universe and the Big Bang was more plausible than the 'Bong!' laden one created by human scientists.

"You remember I said I could go forward and back along the timeline?" said Limantour, "I suspect you can too, now that your Intervention has happened. If we hold hands then I can protect you. We will both be able to hop forward, or else I'll be blocked whilst I am holding on to you."

This fascinated me because I felt no different and could otherwise have taken many decades to realise, I had a new power.

300

"Okay, Limantour, you'll have to explain?"

Limantour looked at me. "I said I could go forward, that I could channel hop to another dimension?"

I nodded.

She looked at me again, "Tomales can also channel hop, and just like I can hold your hands to take you with me, so can Tomales. It is how we found out about the ways to bypass the End."

Limantour continued, "And now, I am sure that it has given you some of the Wakener powers since your Intervention. You might not know it yet, but you should be able to slide forwards and backwards along the time-line."

"But only backwards to where I was given the powers?" I asked.

"Yes, to when you Intervened. But it is why I want to hold you when we go forward the first time. To protect you and to ensure we can get back."

I understood. Although I didn't feel any different, like after a human has a flu jab, I now had extra powers.

"Shall we do this thing?" asked Limantour, she held my hands ever so gently and I felt the familiar fast-forward of a time jump.

I looked around and could see that the area was different from the original Wilmington, Delaware. There were none of the familiar automobiles, and there seemed to be new transportation provided by Pod-like structures which seemed to run on guided paths.

The cityscape was also different, with slab-sided glassy tower blocks replacing the low rise of the older city. I realised that moving forward in a developed economy was vastly different from moving forward across older times.

Limantour spoke again, "Interesting. We have now passed the old endpoint. Your Intervention must have created a new path for Earth."

"How far did we jump?" I asked.

"Oh, maybe 300 years and still at the same location. Far less than we've been jumping in olden times."

I felt the floor shift very slightly. I'd always been aware of my gravity sensitivity, which was something like a human child's sense of balance on snow-skis. I was aware that I was making a very slight balance correction, beyond the normal one I'd associate with the pull of the moon.

Limantour looked at me, "What are you thinking?" she asked.

"I don't know, I said, but it feels almost as if there are two moons, both exerting some kind of gravity onto Earth."

"Yes, there are," answered Ed Tomales, "The second moon has been created by humankind, and is used to launch space missions outside of Earth's atmosphere."

By now it was early evening, and she pointed into the

darkening sky. "See," she said, "There is the moon and to its left in the sky is Moon 2, smaller but also in a geocentric orbit. It is much closer than the moon, but is on a similar rotation to the moon, in the Outer Van Allen belt."

But I thought that was dangerous?" I asked.

"Not if the Moon 2 is positioned in the safe slot, " answered Tomales,

"The gap between the inner and outer Van Allen belts is caused by the Very Low Frequency (VLF) waves, which scatter particles, and which result in the gain of particles to the atmosphere. Solar outbursts can pump particles into the gap, but they drain again in a matter of days, " answered Limantour.

I could see that Limantour and Tomales had this worked out.

Tomales approached me, "We have something else to do here."

"But I thought my Intervention was complete? I mean, I sent out two gravity waves?"

"It is," said Limantour., "Any of us can do this next part. Tomales has obtained the number that we need to pass on."

I was intrigued. We had somehow leapt forward into a new zone, called 'New Delaware,' and the effects of the knowledge shards appeared to be already in full swing. What could we possibly need another code for?

Tomales showed me a hand communicator. It was from

the place we had left and I wasn't sure if it would still work, realising that it would need legacy technology to communicate with anything else.

Tomales had already pressed a transmit button and I could hear a sound like a faint bell ringing.

Then I heard a click and someone answered, "Hello," said a faint female voice, "who are you?"

"You will need to hold it to your ear," explained Tomales loudly.

"Ah,' said the voice, "It is vintage. Like an old telephone."

Tomales had put her device into speaker mode, and we could now all hear the distant voice more clearly.

"Hi Cindy," said the Tomales, " I know you are with Sam now. The reason we are using this old device is because it operates on frequencies that are no longer used for routine communications. It gives us an advantage in that we can talk without the risk of being monitored."

I was completely out of my depth now. I did not know what Tomales was talking about, nor to whom she was speaking

Tomales continued, "We would like to meet you to discuss what you have found in the envelope. It is from two of your distant colleagues. Like you, they have identified some anomalies with the work on Ganymede. There are some major forces in play."

Cindy asked, "So how do you know about us, and how do you know about this? Have you been following me?

Have you been listening to my conversations?"

"Only in so far as it is in your best interests," said Tomales, "We don't want to snoop, but there are some things we will need to find out."

"You also said I was in danger?" said Cindy. "How do I know the danger isn't from you?"

"You're right," said Tomales, "But the truth is we think you have discovered something, and we need to follow it up as a lead toward a bigger situation."

"But you seem to imply that we made some mistakes?" said Cindy, "Other people have been taken away from their workplaces because they found similar anomalies to me but then extrapolated the wrong conclusions."

"Possibly," said Tomales, "But we think they are probably closer to what is happening than even you are."

Cindy answered, "If you expect me to cooperate, I will want Sam to also be involved."

"That's fine," said Tomales, "We wanted you both."

"And what assurances do I have that if I talk to you further face-to-face, that it won't get me into other difficulties?" asked Cindy.

"I can't give you any guarantees," said Tomales, "But I think our approach so far has been trustworthy. As I said, we want to understand what is happening on Ganymede."

"So where are you taking this conversation?" Asked another voice, which I took to be Sam.

Tomales remained silent.

Cindy repeated the question, "Where are you taking this?"

Tomales answered, "Sam, you need to remember that this is an old communicator, and it limits the voice sensitivity unless you are very close to its microphone.

"We want to meet with you, and to show you some things about Ganymede. There is some risk, so we will need to take precautions in how we meet you."

"Just a moment," said Cindy, "I need to check with Sam about this."

"They want us to go somewhere with them," I could hear Cindy speaking to Sam, "They say they want to tell us something about what is happening and why they have taken the information about the ship."

There was a pause whilst Sam considered this.

"Okay, let's say we go with you," he said. We could hear him pick up the communicator and the sound suddenly became louder.

"Let's say we go with you; will we meet somewhere fairly close to here and how will we know you're not putting us into danger?"

Tomales answered, "All I can say is that I think you will be in less danger by working with us than if you try to continue as if nothing had happened. "

Tomales continued, "You should look for a Sven

Mallinson. He'd like you to meet you now so that we can continue this conversation."

"Okay," said Sam, "If we agree, how would we do this?"

"I can get a pod to you where you are," said Tomales, "It will be unmanned but can bring you to a safe location where we can talk."

"It really is in your best interests," Tomales added, speaking softly, "We can walk away from this now and leave you to run with this alone. Working with me and the others, you stand a better chance."

Sam spoke to Cindy, "They want us to go with them now for a meeting. They are prepared to send us a pod to take us there."

Cindy replied, "There seems to be more downside for us if we don't follow this."

Sam spoke back to the communicator, "Okay, I guess you know where we are right now. Send your pod and we will come to meet you."

"Look over to the pod bays. The pod flashing, XTZ 564 is yours. Just get in and it will bring you to us. And bring this communicator with you."

We could hear Sam walking toward the pod bays. Then the sound of climbing into a pod. The communicator had acted as a digital key and the door opened as he approached. Then we heard the pod door closing, and the pod manoeuvring. According to Tomales, they were speeding towards north New Delaware, towards the boundary zone that separated the space zone from the rest of Amerika.

"Okay," I said, "How did you know those people, and to do that? How did you set it up?"

Limantour answered, "Tomales has the ability to look forward through time. She has already visited this area. She knew that the two known as Sam and Cindy would be here and they would need an escape route to get them to a certain other location. We simply had to join the dots. It is where Pod XTZ 564 came in. Tomales had pre-programmed it to go to the next location to support Sam and Cindy. They are both being hunted by some ruthless people, but we can help them. Look, I'll show you around this area."

She gestured toward the nearby transit system, and we all clambered into a pod. I had never used this form of transit before and didn't know what to expect.

"It's okay," said Tomales, "Best to go in this rather than be seen out in the open."

The pod had blanked its windows as we started the journey. By human standards the pods travelled fast, although to a Watcher it was still very slow. Now the pod had slowed right down, and the glass cleared. We all looked out.

"It's horrible," I said, "Like some kind of Armageddon."

"Yes, and the pod has slowed right down to traverse this area," answered Limantour, "It can only mean it must run extra surveillance."

We could see industrial rubble stretching away as far as the eye could see. Some tall posts rose through the rubble, and atop them were video surveillance systems.

A few drones hovered over the landscape, which looked arid and hot.

We passed several gantries with cameras pointing inside of the pod.

"I see, they have partly slowed down to scan us incoming," said Tomales.

Razor wire had been draped around and there were several laser-triggered alert systems.

"We are most definitely heading for the Scratch," said Tomales.

Once we had flickered into this time period, our memories had been backfilled with relevant information. We all knew that the Scratch was a zone just outside of the New Delaware boundaries. It extended for around 10 km in a ragged line around most of the exit points from New Delaware. Like the ramshackle towns that had developed beyond many areas of military installation, the Scratch population centres were at the gates exiting from New Delaware.

Right at the border, there were many layers of security to stop people from getting into New Delaware. Just outside of this was the zone where many people had tried to get in but had then stopped and instead tried to make an opportunistic living around the borders.

The area had become known as the Scratch. It was thought the name came from the phrase 'To scratch a living'. This close to the border was a rough area and didn't have many people passing through unless they were bound in or out of New Delaware. Nowadays it was a label on a ramshackle microclimate filled with rough-necks looking for ways to make a turn on what was happening inside the space zone.

Uniformed new Delaware residents were usually safe because everyone knew they had full identity tracking and anyone interfering with them would be rapidly traceable.

The New Delaware Security Force would swoop into the Scratch at the first sign of trouble affecting New Delaware residents and bring the full force of their law to bear.

This almost 'take no prisoners' policy meant that the Scratch residents would keep a distance from New Delaware residents.

The same didn't apply to those from the rest of Amerika who passed through the Scratch. NDSF security forces also paid little attention to anything affecting Amerikan residents entering the Scratch. The assumption was that these people would only go forward knowingly.

It suited the New Delaware Security Forces to have this buffer zone because it acted as insulation for the Space Zone.

I noticed the pod had progressively dimmed its windows during this latter part of the journey. This has happened faster than the change in daylight, but I knew that the pod had also put up its protective shields across its windows.

I could also feel a very slight vibration from the pod on the last part of the journey. The pods were self-levelling but on extreme terrain it was possible to sense that there was an un-made route being used.

"We've left the main transit route," said Tomales.

"Yes, yes, I know," said Limantour, "We are going deeper into the Scratch."

 Suddenly there was a click and the door on Tomales' side of the pod cleared. A light appeared, and then the door swung overhead as the pod settled into a docking bay.

"Amber conditions," said the pod.

"Pod explain," asked Limantour.

"Amber condition, uncharted territory, zone alert for outside of New Delaware. Repeat. Uncharted territory, zone alert for outside of New Delaware."

 "Okay," said Tomales, "I'll go first."

She climbed past Limantour and out of the pod. We were all suddenly in a clean and modern complex; not at all like I was expecting.

Inject

"Okay, " I said, "I need some explanations!"

Limantour spoke, "It's like we discussed back at Point Reyes. Earth was reaching its endpoint. We were helpless to watch. Then Tomales went forward and used her ability to hop into another dimension. She met Holden, and he showed her that there was a way forward. She brought back the information, and we set up the Intervention.

Tomales added, "Holden's plan, supported by Abbott, had two parts; to show a discovery of magnetite from Hubble Four and then to bring in knowledge useful to Earth to exploit it. Holden retrieved the knowledge shards from another dimension and then your gravity wave caused them to wash up in sight of Earth."

I nodded. So far, I had understood.

"But how has the knowledge spread so fast and how is it I already know some much about this time?"

Limantour continued, "I can't say exactly how the knowledge of magnetomics spread so fast throughout the scientific community. Holden told us it was using nematocysts from Chrysaora - jellyfish stings injecting knowledge to the humans."

Tomales added, "Yes, Holden had brought these knowledge artefacts from another dimension. Their use on Earth is unpredictable. I didn't know that it would affect us as Watchers, for example."

She added, "Your other knowledge gain does not differ from when you have done forward jumps before. It's just that there is so much more that has occurred this time. The Great Leap they are calling it."

Limantour continued, "Now we are in the newly created and saved version of the Earth. Remember, we have jumped forward three hundred years. Earth now understands magnetite and has created a mining programme which runs between Earth and Ganymede, a moon of Jupiter. They are using partially machine-based robots - androids if you will - to pilot, operate and mine the distant moon. There has also been a technology shift between Earth and Ganymede, which is now considerably ahead of Earth."

"But what about Holden?" I asked, "He was trying to take over and run things?"

"It is a partial success," answered Tomales, "Earth has formed three super-powers which together operate an Earth Council. They are America, Eurussia and Sino-Nihon."

Tomales continued, "On Ganymede and its Earthside infrastructure support, there are zones run by different closed communities. The Eurussian zone, the Amerikan Mafia zone, and an area operated by a mix of Chinese and Japanese called Sino-Nihon and run by the Japanese Yakuza. We are currently close to the Space Zone of Amerika."

"But that suggests that gangsters run the entire mining operation?" I asked.

Limantour answered, "Mining, Manufacturing and Infrastructure augmented by robotics and nano-systems. Here, Earthside, the entire New Delaware facility is run by Torus industries, once known as Raven. They had seen through the acceleration of the space program to support Ganymede. They were a consolidation of several other companies, including Biotree, which had developed much of the nanotechnology prevalent on Ganymede and Earthside.

Tomales added, "There are two other equivalent huge corporations operating in other parts of the world. AlfaCorporatsiya (AlfaCorp) for Eurussia and Kăxīmŭ gōngyè (Cassim Gongje) for Sino-Nihon."

"Is this what they call an Unintended Consequence from my Intervention?" I asked.

"Kinda," said Limantour, "But remember that there wouldn't even be an Earth without our intervention."

I also realised I was now too close to this unfolding situation. As a Watcher I should remain detached - on the outside - but I felt as if I was inside of these events.

Arbitrary

"We must go!" said Limantour, suddenly," We'll exceed the maximus here in this version of Earth."

 I looked at Tomales, who was nodding, "Yes, we need to get back to our familiar unspooling of events - we are in a metaverse which could be unstable. If we get arbitrarily shifted to new locations, it could now be as far away as Moon 2, or even Ganymede"

Tomales continued, "The good news is that you'll keep the knowledge of this outcome, if we go back to the time of your Intervention, Farallon. And when we go forward under normal conditions, it should lead to this future. One we are now prepared for."

With that, Tomales took my hand and that of Limantour and we jumped back to the time and place just after the Intervention. We were back at the Travbane Racetrack, in Bodø, Norway. Drake looked over.

"You've only been gone for a matter of minutes!" he said.

"It's okay," said Limantour, "We've reset our time here, we'll be good for a complete maximus again. Another 5 hours together here in Bodø. But Drake you'll need to leave soon."

"Only after you tell me what you discovered," he said.

"So, we've just visited a new version of Earth's timeline," I said, "Where our Intervention has worked."

Tomales continued, "Yes, and that is because of your gravity wave, the second one, which washed the results of Holden's preparations across from another metaverse into our one. Earth has gained the science to make small powerful motors, tiny, long-lasting batteries from magnetite, advanced healthcare via the Tropus and nano-engineering and an apparent uplift in robotics knowledge."

"It's a lot, but is that everything?" I asked.

"No, I don't think so," said Tomales, "I've travelled further along that timeline that we were on. The Intervention transferred some mind manipulations as well, and some powerful new weapons. It seems that Holden's plan for control of Earth has also been to block part of it. A large part of the Southern hemisphere will be partially erased from Earthside memory. Some entire countries will go. An exclusion zone will be created and at the boundary, some high-powered weapons installed to prevent transgressions."

"Has this happened yet?" asked Drake, looking like he was keeping up with the conversation.

"No, but it happens quickly," answered Tomales, "First the tropus and a new cartridge delivery system for all humans to use. These cartridge systems become a proprietary money spinner for Brant, then Raven and finally Torus. Everyone on earth needs the tropus and it must be renewed every month. Think of the income stream."

Drake added, "Yes, the comms I have been monitoring are already talking about them. Apparently, some of the major Research & Development for the programme has been run from here in Bodo."

Limantour added, "Once the cartridge system is in place, it can also be used as a delivery system for the nano-engineered machines which become responsible for certain health care maintenance. And of course, there are degraded versions too - below standard clones that can be used as cheap substitutes for the real thing."

"You knew all of this?" I asked Tomales, "Yet you still let me go?"

Tomales replied, "No, actually I could see none of this until you Intervened and broke through the blockage which was preventing us all from looking into the future. You can see it all too now that you have moved from Watcher to a more proactive status."

"But what about Abbott?" I asked, "Would he have known about any of this?"

"Probably, but he chose not to share it," said Limantour, "I guess he wanted to stay on the right side of Holden."

On cue, Abbott reappeared. It was as if I only needed to say his name and he would appear.

Swirling chaotic waters

Abbott spoke, "You have all played your part now. Holden is pleased and may seek you for other roles later. You see what this has done?"

I answered Abbot, "No, beyond bringing the new attributes across from the other metaverse, I can't see anything else."

"Well, you have answered one of the 13-billion-year-old questions. That of creation. Most religious systems have positioned this. As an example, the Egyptians had several creation myths."

Abbott continued, "All the Egyptian ones begin with the swirling chaotic waters, called Nun. Amun-Ra, the supreme Sun god, willed himself into being, and then created a hill. Amun-Ra possessed an all-seeing eye. He spat out a son, Shu, god of the air, and then a daughter, Tefnut, goddess of moisture.

"These two gods were charged with the task of creating order out of chaos. Shu and Tefnut produced Geb, the Earth with all its natural landforms and life, excluding humans, and Nut, the sky and celestial bodies.

"Geb lifted Nut above him and gradually the world came into order, but Shu and Tefnut became lost in the remaining darkness.

"Amun-Ra removed his all-seeing eye and sent it to search for them. When Shu and Tefnut returned, thanks to the eye, Amun-Ra wept with joy.

"Where the tears struck the Earth, humans began to form."

"But there is only good news from this story?" I asked, "No Heaven and Hell?"

"That's right," said Abbott, "You have to look further to find the darkness."

Like in the Quran?" asked Tomales.

Limantour answered, "Even the light and darkness of night and day came together with good will."

Abbot nodded, "Yes, in the Islamic religion from the Middle East in the seventh century CE, the Quran states Allah created the Sun, the Moon and the planets, including the Earth. Allah also created the night and the day.

"Originally, the heavens and the Earth were joined as one unit, before they were ripped apart. Following a big explosion, Allah 'turned to the sky, and it had been as smoke.'

"He said to the sky and the Earth: 'Come together, willingly or unwillingly.' They said: 'We come together in willing obedience.' As a result, the elements and what was to become the planets and stars cooled, came together, and formed shapes, following the natural laws that Allah established in the Universe.

"The first human beings, Adam and his wife Eve (Hawwah), appear in the Quran, which states that they were created from clay, and were brought to life by the blowing of the soul into their bodies.

"It's the same all over the planet," said Limantour.

"The Sumerian Mesopotamian creation myth involves a struggle of the younger god Marduk, against the chaotic water gods; the male Apsu, representing fresh water and the female Tiamat, representing salt water. A cycle of violence then erupts, resulting in Marduk, the aggressive upstart, leading the gods to a final decisive battle against Tiamat.

"Marduk defeats Tiamat and splits her body, creating heaven and Earth. The moral of this Mesopotamian myth is that the human being is an insignificant part of a much larger struggle within the natural world; and that there is a monumental struggle between order and disorder."

"Order and disorder. Now we are getting somewhere," I said.

Abbott continued, "Then there was the Zoroastrian religion of Ancient Persia, in which the world was created by the deity, Ahura Mazda. The great mountain Alburz grew for 800 years until it touched the sky. From that point, rain fell, forming the Vourukasha sea and two great rivers.

"The first animal to be created, the white bull, lived on the bank of the river Veh Rod. However, the evil spirit Angra Mainyu, killed it. Its seed was carried to the Moon and purified, creating many animals and plants.

"Across the river lived the first man, Gayomard. He was as bright as the Sun. Angra Mainyu also killed him. But the Sun purified his seed for forty years, which then grew into Masha and Mashyanag, the first human mortals. There's more cannibalism in this story, but do you see, Farallon, conflict leads to a stable outcome.?"

Tomales asked, "I'm not sure what you are trying to prove here? Do you imply new conflict before the Earth settles again?"

Abbot answered, "We can look at Central African, Maori, Viking, Japanese and Aztec origins and they all show humans born out of a suffering or conflict. As an example, the giant pale god, Mbombo, a white-coloured figure who had been ill for millions of years in Africa but then brought the Sun the Moon, stars and nine animals, from which all other descend; Or the Vikings Odin, Vili and Ve, who killed the primordial frost giant Ymir and made his body into parts of the Universe; Japan with Izanagi and Izanami gliding down the rainbow-striped floating bridge of heaven, stirring the water but Izanami dying after giving birth to the fire god Ho-musubi. In Aztec beliefs, Huitzilopochtli, the God of War and the Sun, sprang from his mother, Coatlicue, fully grown and armoured. He attacked Coyolxauhqui, killing her with the aid of a fire serpent and so appeared the Moon."

" I could go on but the pattern is a coda of illness and death followed by the recognition of the Universe and the dawn of humanity. We all know that the Universe goes back much further than these humans, and so their beliefs are surrounded by what they know. The main symphony finishes before they are allowed their embellishments."

I thought Abbott was speaking some sense but wondered about a punchline.

As if on cue, Abbott continued, "So, to make an omelette, you have to break a few eggs."

I groaned. Next, he'd be quoting that revolution is not a dinner party. But deep down I knew he signalled that the restart of Earth might be surrounded by some form of conflict. Conflict introduced by Holden's wish to attain control.

I looked over to Limantour and Tamales. Their expressions were like mine. I think they had both been duped and I could see they were trying to think of ways to remedy the situation. But of course, the world was entirely different now that a slice of another reality had entered.

Complexity and entropy

I began to realise that by crossing some artefacts from an alternate reality into our own metaverse, we had just thrown another layer of complexity across the Earth.

All societies need to create some meaning for the natural world around them and their existence. Without scientific evidence, they develop mythical creation stories traditionally passed down orally from one generation to another. An earthquake, storm, volcanic eruption, famine or pandemic pestilence, was often believed to be the sign of an angry god.

These creation stories were powerful and acted as the glue which embedded the people with a common purpose and within their respective cultures.

Then, with the passing of time, we see the added thresholds of complexity.

This may seem at odds with the second law of thermodynamics in physics, which states that the total entropy or disorder in the Universe will increase over space and time.

If that's true, and the Universe is getting constantly more disordered, then why do we see ordered things like galaxies, stars, planets and complex life, like humans? In physics there is a difference between complexity and entropy.

Entropy refers to the number of ways matter and energy can be re-arranged within a relatively stable system, in this case, the Universe. It is possible for something to grow in complexity and yet become less disordered at the same time.

Typically, as entropy increases, disorder also increases, reaching a peak and then decreasing again. But within this large disorder are pockets of ordered complexity.

This is where we will find galaxies, stars, planets and life in all of its complexity and diversity.

In the beginning, the Universe had little entropy and was very simple and homogenous. As the Universe expanded, it became more complex despite the greater disordered entropy.

At the end of its existence, the Universe will become simple again, as all the galaxies and stars exhaust matter and energy, and disordered entropy becomes extremely high during this process of the Universe contracting and "dying."

But the wash from the alternative metaverse means there will still be a long time for this to unspool. It felt like we had just added some new glitter into the equation.

Naval

In Hinduism, which also originated in India sometime between 2,300 and 1,500 BCE, it is believed that the world is created many times, repeatedly, and not just once and for all.

Hinduism also states that this Universe is one of many multiple universes in existence, with other forms of life abounding and existing on different planes.

In the Hindu religion, the creation story from the Vishnu Purana states that Vishnu, while laying on an ocean of milk on top of the serpent Sesha, sprung a lotus from his navel that contained the god Brahma.

Having been sprung from Vishnu's navel, Brahma created all living things including humans, as well as the Sun, Moon, planets and several other gods and demigods.

Now that's a far-sighted idea and seems to organise some of the thinking. Multiple planes of existence. The 'branes and their metaverses. Humans, animals, and other entities. Maybe even Watchers?

PART FOUR

Versatility at the Crossroads

I could tell we were at a crossroads. This is where adversity favours the versatile.

I thought back through the times I had experienced. From two million years ago, as tree-living African hominids attempted to live on two feet after cold, dry weather attacked their forests.

The open grasslands that resulted made it imperative to run and hunt and see into the distance, which resulted in *Homo erectus*, an important early version of humanity, with a brain around two-thirds the size of a 21st Century brain. The versatile walk tall.

Homo erectus, ranged far out of Africa and evolved first into the bigger-brained *Homo heidelbergensis*—people who were hunting and making axes in England half a million years ago, and had a brain not so much smaller than ours, around 1,200 grams compared with our 1,500.

This picture of human development is a brutal simplification. Scientists name and slot them into neat divisions, and assemble evolutionary trees, but the truth was messier.

What most needs to be grasped is that modern humans were not just a single super-bright, planet-conquering ape, who leapt as if by magic from an earlier world belonging to dim ape-men.

Those earlier species, including the famous Neanderthals, and in Asia the 'Denisovans' also survived dramatic changes in climate and pushed into new territories as pioneers, equipped with cutting- and killing-tools.

They decorated themselves, had a language, and interbred with the newcomers, *Homo sapiens*.

Humankind, as we know them in the 21st Century, had arrived.

Peer inside

This is how it works
You're young until you're not
You love until you don't
You try until you can't
You laugh until you cry
You cry until you laugh
And everyone must breathe
Until their dying breath

No, this is how it works
You peer inside yourself
You take the things you like
And try to love the things you took
And then you take that love you made
And stick it into some
Someone else's heart
Pumping someone else's blood

And walking arm in arm
You hope it don't get harmed
But even if it does
You'll just do it all again

Regina Spektor

We'll always have Paris

Now we are in Casablanca, Morocco, sitting in an old courtyard-style mansion built against the walls of the Old Medina. The seafood restaurant and piano bar is filled with architectural and decorative details: curved arches, a sculpted bar, balconies, balustrades and beaded and stencilled brass lighting and plants that cast luminous shadows on white walls.

This was Limantour's idea again, and I knew that she'd chosen somewhere that resembled a film set. I sensed she was about to make another suggestion.

The air rippled, and Tomales appeared.

I wanted to say, "Of all the gin joints in all the towns in all the world, she walks into mine," but Tomales hadn't walked in. She'd rematerialized.

Instead, a "Hi Tomales!" but Tomales replied, "We'll always have Paris!" so I guess there is some justice in this human world.

"Will Drake join us?" I asked.

"Any moment," answered Tomales, and then, with a quiet crack, Drake appeared and was almost instantly sipping a cocktail. "Cheers, " he said, then looked at me, he raised his glass, "Here's looking at you, kid."

I worked out that they must have had a pre-meeting about whatever we were to discuss.

Limantour looked at me.

"Farallon," she said. Limantour speaking my name again could only mean that something intense was to follow.

"Farallon. This is how it works. You've successfully created the Intervention. Both parts. The seen part, and an equally important unseen aspect."

She paused for effect, then continued, "Holden has engineered for unseen artifacts from another dimension to accompany the ones helpful to humankind. The knowledge shards also contained something else, which we are sure has something to do with his attempt to win power."

I sensed the dark-side dragon slither across my body, like the time we were on the beach at Point Reyes.

She continued, "Abbott will assist him and we think there are others, too. Tomales has gone forward along this timeline and seen that it could be as long as three hundred years before this plays out."

Limantour spoke, "And if you say to me tomorrow, 'Oh what fun it all would be.' Then what's to stop us, Farallon?"

I could see what she was doing.

Tomales spoke. "Yes, and there seem to be a couple of future outcomes as well. Heavily influenced by what is and what should never be."

I spoke, "But the wind won't blow and we really shouldn't go. It only goes to show, we must take our time."

Drake added, "Yes. I have checked communications and Earth gets Trigax weapons, blood management, nano-engineering and new cyber robotics. It learns to mine magnetite and how to craft new miniature power units to save the earth from a climate catastrophe. There are wars along the way, including a terrible Klima War, which decimates the Earthside population. Shortly after this, Holden gets a foothold towards power."

"What do you want?" I asked.

They looked at one another, then Limantour spoke. "We think that we four can divert this from a catastrophe."

"How?" I asked, fearing the worst.

"We are now all Wakeners, still with our special powers. We have stepped beyond being Watchers and are now in the proactive world of Wakeners. It means we can move along the timeline. It also means that we can adopt a human persona."

"I'm confused," I said, "How can this be?"

"In the new world with its intersect with an alternative reality, we can adopt Personas from another's Presence. Here is our proposal."

My mind was whirring. This was becoming too much to comprehend.

Limantour continued, "Drake has been running an

analysis of the players in the next section of this. People who directly or indirectly interact with Holden. He has made a list of Candidates."

"Candidates?" I asked.

"Yes, people or other points at which we can insert Wakeners to take over the actions of the original actors."

I wasn't sure what I'd just heard. Did it mean that as a Wakener, I could slip into someone else's personality? Become them?

"It is supposed to be a technology for use with cybernetics," explained Tomales, "It is not even due to be discovered for another 60 years, but because we went forward 300 years and have retrieved the residual knowledge, we know about things that are yet to be. However, this cybernetic transformation can also work with Wakeners, who can add themselves to anyone, not just cyborgs.

Limantour added an explanation, "Wakeners know to exploit the darkness when humans sleep. In 5 hours of their darkness, we can exchange considerable memories with them. We need five nights to completely exchange everything."

"What does it mean?" I asked, still confused.

"It means, after five nights tuned into a sleeping human, we will have enough power to completely inhabit them. They will still have everything they had previously, including free will, but we will examine everything from their perspective and in extreme situations give them insights from our vastly more complete knowledge."

"But that sounds like the jewel wasp," I said, "the one that paralyses cockroaches and then enslaves them to support the wasp's own life cycle?"

"Not at all," said Limantour, "This is benign - we are using the host human as a means to an end, sure enough, but only in the best interests of humanity. They won't even be aware that they are being supported."

I realised that since we had washed the alternative metaverse fragments into Earth, things had taken an altogether unpredictable turn.

I asked, "You say 'we'. Who exactly do you mean?"

Limantour answered, "All of us. Tomales, Drake, me and you."

"We've worked it out. Here," Limantour showed me a fragment of paper.

I read it:

- *Farallon becomes Scrive Mallinson.* An experienced ex-military freelancer based in London
- *Limantour becomes Chantel.* Madcap adventure-seeker London socialite.
- *Tomales becomes Charlie.* Gambler and mercenary based in New York.
- *Drake becomes Nathan.* Security specialist in Bodo, Norway

There was not much to go on.

"How can this possibly work?" I asked.

Limantour answered, "Don't you see? You have turned from a Watcher into a Wakener. You'll be able to act now, and not only that, but you'll also carry the knowledge of the future from your trip forward with Tomales and I. Your mind has been loaded with the next 300 years of developments."

"But what is the downside?" I asked.

"1 You'll be linked into a specific human. They operate slowly, so you'll have to get used to that, although you can help them at our normal speed of thought and knowledge."

"2 You'll need to get used to travel at a human rate. No hops to another position on the earth."

"3 You will need to take care of your human. They are not immortal like us, and our persistence is interrupted if they are killed. You'll still be able to get back to the Wakener dimension though."

"4 You'll need to resist some of the human emotional traits. It can be like a massive sensory overload when you start."

"5 All of your Wakener back-channels will go, although you will still have a powerful affinity for each of us and we will gravitate toward one another."

Limantour paused. I could understand each of the points. To be honest, it felt like a useful break from the billions of years acting as a Watcher. I was ready for this, even if it tied one hand behind my back.

Tomales reminded me, "You will be on a 300-year journey, but you will need to experience all of it. It won't be like now when you can jump forward to avoid some tedium."

Limantour added, "Yes, but nearly the entire time will be packed with human-level adventure and decisions. It won't be dull!"

"It is tonight," said Drake, "When the humans are sleeping, we will enter their minds. Our Personas will interact with their Presence. They will awaken, feel little different but have all the augmented knowledge and speed that we bring to them."

"Do we have to come to a special laboratory?" I asked, "Like some kind of movie scene?"

"No, " said Drake, "You'll be linked by precognition. A perceptual ability that allows the acquisition of non-inferential information arising from a future point in spacetime. As Watchers we have been bestowed with the Multiphasic Model of Precognition (MMPC). In the physics domain, this addresses the question of retro-causation and how it is possible for information to traverse from one spacetime point to another."

I'd temporarily forgotten that Drake was a geek.

He continued, "Then, the second method is from the neuroscience domain, which addresses the acquisition and interpretation of retro causal signals across three stages:

"(a) perception of signals from an information carrier, based on psychophysical variability in a putative signal transducer.

"(b) cortical processing of the signals, mediated by a

cortical hyper-associative mechanism; and

"(c) cognition, mediated by normal cognitive processes, leading to a response based on retro causal information."

To my surprise, my brain was keeping up with this, like it had received an upgrade during its 300-year-round trip.

Drake continued, "If I put this simply, we just need to target the right individuals and start the transfer, which will end after around five human sleep periods."

In five days and nights, I would be completely operating from within my target. In this case, someone named Scrive Mallinson.

"How will it work?" I asked, "...How do we start this?"

"Oh, It's already started," said Limantour, smiling.

Scrive

So now I was Scrive. I clicked a new cartridge into place in my forearm and felt the cold rush snake from my arm to burst somewhere inside my head. These were entirely new sensations to me.

Next, I checked the small plexi-inspection window briefly and could see my blood already changing from a bright red back to orange, and I knew that within another twenty minutes it would again be the safe yellow colour.

I seemed to know that red blood spelled danger, and I had been careless to let Scrive's system deplete its supply of the tropus for so long.

I could feel the pulse bubbling on the left side of my head above the eye-line. I knew this was my body regaining its equilibrium. I squeezed both hands into a fist shape the way I, Scrive, had been taught and used my two middle fingers to massage the fleshy areas below my thumbs while the system adjusted.

This cartridge was having a vastly stronger effect on my sense of being, compared with the transfer of my Farallon Persona into Scrive's Presence. I could know that I, Farallon, was now operating from within Scrive. That I, Farallon, could bestow great knowledge and powers onto Scrive.

Another five minutes, and I was walking across Chelsea Bridge to the Tube station. I was operating on Scrive's internal logic, living as a human. Scrive lived less than ten minutes on foot from the nearest transit stop, and his ride to today's meeting was around fifteen minutes. I could feel the cartridge working, and a relaxed acceptance of the day's tasks was already returning.

Scrive looked briefly toward the sky. A jagged spark had flicked across. Now gentle vapour trails were crawling behind what had been a brief tear shooting along the path of the River Thames.

Others walked at a similar pace towards the station, although Scrive ducked to the right into a quieter street that also cut a corner and missed some traffic crossings.

I glanced as I prepared to cross the diagonal into the station and glimpsed someone I recognised.

She had a petite almost boyish build, dressed in black, dark hair in a black band. Scrive had noticed her for three days now, at the same spot, the same pace, and the same appearance. I knew she would look up and I'd see the small tattoo by her left eye. At least I assumed it was a tattoo and not consistently applied daily make-up. As she passed, I thought I could hear her gently humming a tune. Maybe from a streamer, but I couldn't see any signs of her wearing one. I wondered if this was another Watcher or Wakener.

I descended into the TfL transit. My new cartridge meant I had a good range on my transceiver and could access the transport system without overtly waving my arm over the sensor. It would take some time to get used to these human forms of transportation.

Most travellers referred to the sensors as 'oysters' although this was a reference to a long-defunct technology, much as the Tube itself was merely a reference to the shape of the original tunnels that formed the original wheel-based transport system.

Scrive used the moving floor system to get to the so-called 'high-speed' transit level and stood for a moment waiting for the next transit pod. I clipped myself into a TPOD seat and punched in my destination. The system was pretty fool proof. My cartridge provided the principal co-ordinates for routine travel, and a short, personalised menu of options had appeared on the screen.

Of course, I could go to other points within my regular routes or pre-authorise other destinations in advance, from the HomeLink system. Today was ordinary, though, or at least that was what I needed to suggest, despite what had happened with the transfer of Persona into Scrive.

Chantal

Chantal was meeting Janie at Canada Water. It was across the River from their planned rendezvous with Lars but would give them a chance to plan how they would handle the session before they met him. It was also a five-minute trip to their planned meeting place so they could be 'in position' quickly.

Chantal arrived in a polka dot bodysuit. Three different colours; shorts, top and jacket. There was little point in being a mistress of chaos if Limantour could not mix it up when cloaked in a human body.

"I took the ears off," Chantal said as she hugged Janie. "And I brought a black topcoat as well in case we need to wear disguises." She pointed into a bag where a black compressed micro-fabric nestled amongst some fashion headgear.

Janie's mood briefly lifted at Chantal's appearance. They'd party together sometimes, and Chantal would usually go for something extravagant. Janie's appearance was more conservative, and today she was wearing a dark business suit.

"Thanks for agreeing to cover this", she said to Chantal. "I'm a little bit worried that this is all getting rather weird."

"I wouldn't miss this for anything. You're about to meet a dishy Swede or something," replied Chantal, with Limantour relishing the new freedom of expression she found as a human.

"He's Norwegian, or says he is," replied Janie. "And it is something to do with the firm and the way they are operating."

"What do you want me to do?" asked Chantal, "Hold your hand or what?"

"The main thing is to cover the situation and to follow my lead if I say anything. I may want him to think that we've spread the word about this, so there's no point in trying to keep it to just the two of us."

"Does he look as if he would be violent?" asked Chantal, making like a karate move.

"I don't think so, but put it this way, I think he could outrun us if it came to a race."

"Okay, so we'll listen to what he has to say and what he asks. I suggest we move from the first location to somewhere else to keep him on his toes, too. If we take him to the end of the walkway, we can grab a taxi and then go almost anywhere".

"Good plan. I suggest we go to Westminster. It's full of police and security so we can get out there and if needed we could easily attract attention."

Janie looked at Chantal.

"I don't think you'd have any trouble doing that,

anyway".

They giggled briefly. Limantour enjoyed the sensation.

"Okay, that way, he can tell us his story while we are in the cab. It will only take a few minutes and put him under pressure to get to the point."

They nodded and walked the short distance to the transit point to Canary Wharf. They would be at Smollensky's on time.

Charlie

Charlie's previous history had a few dubious moments when she was raiding high roller casinos by reprogramming the payout software. It had to be undetectable to the house, and Charlie had created a small device to fire the software changes into the system. Tomales secretly approved of this method and the gains that Charlie had made.

Scrive knew about Charlie in Vegas. He helped her get out of trouble when she was in danger of being caught. He'd shown her how to mess up the electronic trail, which had previously led back to her. Now I was linked, already as Scrive, to Charlie as Limantour I this strange layout of the known world.

Charlie spoke, "I took the Casino injector and produced a sub-scale version. It's a lot easier now than when I built the original because of the improved scanner resolutions available. I could use laser light to improve the sensitivity and then fire the new software into the bots, in much the same way that the old version fired software into the Casino devices."

"NSA hadn't seen anything like this before, and they've asked me to show them a breakdown of how it works. I'm heading for CERN to show them in detail. It is my comeuppance for the damage I caused when I was testing the bots I'd been building, and they kept failing and destroying one another.

She pointed to a small titanium box with an elaborate digital lock. "There," she said. "the Nano injector is in the box. It's loaded with 'nanoreductives'. They are my attempt to rebrand the dud nanobots which self-destruct one another!"

"Its' not a bug, it's a feature," smiled Scrive. He looked quizzically at the lock.

"Birthday?" he asked.

"Yes", replied Charlie, "Plus 666 - I wanted to add an edge to this devilish device."

Scrive knew the box would destroy its contents if the wrong number was entered. But knowing Charlie, there would be a twist.

"Yes - birthday will open it but destroy the loader logic. Birthday plus 666 will open it and keep the device intact"

"What about anything else?"

"Three goes and thar she blows," smiled Charlie. "I thought I'd give a pirate hacker a sporting chance."

"Are you getting paid?"

"Yes and no," came the reply. "I should be, but I'm sort of paying off the cost of the destruction I created at Biotree with my hack. But now it's your turn. What are you working with at the moment? I assume it is still with Biotree?"

"Direct at the moment. And big. The biggest probably.

Corny as it may sound if I tell you then you might be in some sort of danger.

"Yeah, right," responded Charlie," As if that would stop me, but first, another refill of the wine?"

Scrive reached across, picked up the wine and gently poured.

"You know what? You might want to help with this. I can split some fees and it is worth it to me to have someone alongside who isn't known to the client. But wait until you hear before you answer."

"I'm intrigued already," said Charlie, ...and fees would be beneficial at the moment."

"Okay, so I've been asked to find out the origin of the cloned Chinese nanobots. There's a leak somewhere and the impact of the copies has collapsed the Biotree share price. I'm supposed to track the leak and pass the information back. Sounds simple, but we are talking about government level conspiracies. Hence the potential danger."

"Wow. This assignment sounds great. I assume the fees are in keeping with the magnitude of the challenge?"

"You know something; I think I could have named any price. I've gone high. The thing that worries me is that they seem almost too happy to accept my terms. It makes me concerned they won't honour the agreement."

"What can you do?"

"I already did it", said Scrive. I negotiated the money in two stages. "all of it now and all of it again when I complete. If I don't, they will come for me and take half back. I don't want that to happen."

"You've already been paid and can get the same again?" asked Charlie, somewhat incredulous.

"Plus, expenses...I said they didn't seem to care about the amount. And don't worry - it's a lot. Come in with me, and I'll split the second amount. You'll be my safeguard that we get paid based upon our successful outcome."

"How much?" asked Charlie.

Scrive told her. It was a huge sum.

Charlie nodded and started to feel like a big prize lottery winner.

Nathan

Nathan was at home with Sheri in Bodø. He looked out of the window, across snow toward some distant hills. Beyond them were mountains. He had grown to love the Norwegian scenery. The water, the sparkling ice and snow. It was like every cliché he'd heard about the place, an extraordinary land where bad vistas were not permitted. Nathan knew that Sheri felt the same. It made the already enjoyable work even better. Sheri had an excellent location, good job, good money and most of all, she was now sharing it all with Nathan.

Although they both worked for Biotree, their roles were very different, and they didn't see each the during the working day. The campus was vast, and they would usually go to work separately, and because of the distance and security inside the facility, it was best to stay out of contact throughout the day. There were ways to communicate, but it was much the same as if they worked in different towns.

Sheri was reading a report on her handheld. It was related to engineering advances in India and the possibility of some breakthroughs in molecular design. Sheri could sense immediately that this wasn't a plausible article. There were holes in the logic, and the approach was one she already knew to be flawed.

Nathan was preparing some food in the kitchen and

called through from time to time to inform of progress. She could tell by the variety of hissing sounds, aromas of onions, garlic and the tell-tale sound of a bottle cork being extracted. Drake, whose Persona was inside of Nathan's Presence, was secretly pleased that Nathan was already a great cook. The evening meal was almost ready.

Sheri knew she had the more demanding and specialised job of the two of them. Her work was at the (almost literally) cutting edge of the design of the nanomachines. Originally, there had been a set of standard assemblies that worked well together. Most of the incremental designs were based around these pieces.

When she explained it to others, she likened it to a car. Four wheels, one on each corner, some seats, an engine, steering and brakes. The nanobots had a similar basic construction kit.

At the small sizes of the machines, it was the use of protein as a fuel and the same effect that makes cream in coffee eventually spread through the liquid that created a bot power source. It also provided a significant physical limitation to the small machines and their deployment. The 'coffee-cup' Brownian motion made everything shake dramatically at this small scale. Nothing was every static and the trick with the scientists was to harness this motion as a power source.

The building blocks that Sheri used were like the components of the car. There were components for movement, components for sensing, components to join things together - the so-called fixtures - like the chassis of a car and elements to provide grip and contact between the machines - the end effectors.

Then, as Nathan referred, "JASMOP" - or "Just a small matter of programming" to create the operating systems for these small devices. Just a small matter was an interesting point. The technology of Scanning Probe Microscopes used to view the assembly work had never really scaled itself and relied upon clean, secure environments and mega-voltages. It was not surprising when a speck of dust would be like throwing a planet at some of these machines.

Sheri's work was within the so-called 'exotics' division. As expected, there were pictures of palm trees and Pina-Coladas stuck to the walls inside, but fundamentally this was the area where Sheri tried to outdo her maker.

It was the place where new elements were designed. Original elements to create the missing shapes of matter needed to extend the constructor kit of parts for the nanomachines. The pieces that God forgot. There were practical physical limitations to how they could be used. Apart from atomic forces that would blast structures apart, the continued jittering from Brownian motion and the protein fuel consumption of the tiny devices, there were still some basic components that were proving impossible to construct. It was like the car but with only a few degrees of steering and no gears.

Sheri and the team were attempting to build the new shapes. The missing piece parts that would extend the nano constructor kit.

Nathan entered the room, triumphant. "Dinner is served!", he quipped and gestured towards their dining table. They would still eat together whenever possible because the nature of the work often meant irregular hours, and this would give a chance to spend some time chatting. There was an inverse luxury to 'dining in'. Most of the time, workers in the facility would avail themselves of the vast eco-system of restaurants and cafes that had established around the complex.

Pretty much all cuisines were catered for, from fast-food Americana to the fanciest French or Japanese food. Most evenings they would eat out, sometimes alone but often in company with others from the facility.

Being alone in their living quarters was an excellent time for decompression, even if Sheri appeared to have started the evening with a scientific journal article.

"I can't believe it's nearly two years that we've been here." stated Nathan. "I know it will be after your birthday that it's officially two years for you and about three weeks later for me."

Sheri alerted herself as Nathan started this line of conversation. A meal at home, talk about how long... would this be leading to a discussion of 'them'? She decided to see where it was going, but Nathan moved in another direction.

"I hope tonight's 'dish of the day' is okay?" he inquired, "I had to scratch around for some ingredients".

Sheri relaxed. She was keen enough for a talk about their future, but tonight it didn't somehow seem to be the time. She was just too strung out on the current work.

A few tonal changes were creating some new upsets. Makatomi's business plans were at odds with Sheri's personal beliefs. Instead of the Biotree being about healthcare and the future, it seemed to move towards more ominous goals. They had recently brought some contractors into Sheri's department who seemed rather more lackadaisical about their approach to safety systems.

"I've been working on some new secure perimeter systems this week," called Nathan," It looks as if Biotree are getting even more paranoid based upon the recent share prices and business news."

Nathan worked in another area of high technology, but rather than being progressive and forward-facing, like the pure R&D that Sheri conducted, this was more related to the protection and security of the Biotree complex. Beyond obvious physical defences, there were rings within rings of security measures that could both give an impression of a relaxed environment but could become extremely strict in moments if something inappropriate was detected.

Nathan worked on the improvements to this world. A guardian role that also meant he spent more time around the whole complex than Sheri.

They had initially met just after Nathan had joined. Sheri had been out for a weekend skiing in the adjoining mountains, with a couple of new-found girlfriends when they had run into an 'induction team' part of which included Nathan.

Sheri was snowboarding at the time and noticed that Nathan seemed similarly adept, and they'd broken away from the group to try a particularly exciting route. At least that was what Nathan had said and - on reflection - Sheri had also thought the course unexpectedly delightful.

They'd been together ever since that first encounter. After a short time, they had moved into what was considered one of the better apartment areas. Their facility looked out to the sea on one side and hills and distant mountains on the other side.

Tonight, Nathan had placed candles outdoors in the Norwegian tradition, and Sheri could see a distant twinkle from boats on the sea and stars in the sky.

But no, tonight wasn't the one to have deep conversations about the future.

Aborigine

After what seemed to them like an eternity, the Sun Mother peeked her head above the horizon in the East. The Earth's children learned to expect her coming and going, and were no longer afraid.

At first the children lived together peacefully, but eventually envy crept into their hearts. They began to argue. The Sun Mother was forced to come down from her home in the sky to mediate the bickering.

She gave each creature the power to change their form to whatever they chose.

However, she was not pleased with the result. The rats she had made, had changed into bats; there were giant lizards and red fish with blue tongues and feet.

The Sun Mother looked down upon the Earth and thought she must create new beings, to not anger the All Spirit.

She gave birth to the Earth, Water, Fire and Air. And then to humans.

Pulse

Follow the timeline for the next 300 years.

Pulse
The immediate sequel.
Features Scrive, Chantal, Charlie and Nathan

And then, 300 years later
Edge
Edge, Blue
Edge, Red